HOLD ME
UNTIL MIDNIGHT

a Grayson Brothers novel

CHRISTINA
PHILLIPS

Entangled Publishing, LLC
2614 South Timberline Road
Suite 109
Fort Collins, CO 80525
Visit our website at www.entangledpublishing.com.

Brazen is an imprint of Entangled Publishing, LLC. For more information on our titles, visit www.brazenbooks.com.

Edited by Candace Havens
Cover design by Heather Howland
Cover art by Shutterstock

Manufactured in the United States of America

First Edition June 2015

an Entangled imprint

For Mark, with love

Chapter One

Scarlett Ashford stared at the dilapidated single story building and her courage faltered. Why was she so nervous? It wasn't the fact she was standing in one of the seediest back streets of downtown Los Angeles — or that the peeling façade boasted up-to-the minute security cameras, as though the occupants expected trouble and were more than happy to confront it.

No, her hands were clammy and her stomach churned because of the appointment she had with one of the owners in exactly three minutes.

She glanced at the weathered sign above the door.

Graysons'.

That was it. Nothing to indicate who or what *Graysons'* might be. They obviously operated purely by word of mouth. Well, wasn't that how she'd heard of them in the first place? Not that anyone knew she'd taken note of the name and address when her work colleagues had been discussing Jackson

Grayson's methods of…persuasion.

She took a step forward and her finger hovered over the entry button. Was she really going through with this? Wouldn't it be much easier to simply fall in with her soon-to-be stepmother's plans? Ever since her dad's heart attack eighteen months ago she'd walked on eggshells around him, afraid that the slightest upset would be disastrous for his health. *"Oh Scarlett's no problem, darling. She's such a malleable little thing. Does anything she's told in the hope of gaining Daddy's approval,"* her father's fiancé had said to a friend on the phone.

It stung. Not because she and Clarissa were close. In fact, she thought Clarissa was a social climbing bitch.

It was the jibe about trying to get her dad's attention. Because Scarlett knew it was true. Her two older brothers did whatever they liked, and Dad boasted about their exploits to anyone who'd listen.

All he wanted from *her* was a couture mannequin. That she was the image of her late mother didn't help. That was the one thing she had in common with her dad. They mourned the premature death of her mom ten years ago. Maybe if she looked more like her dad, he'd see her as an individual.

Never going to happen.

She straightened her spine and jabbed the button. *I'm more than a pale imitation of Mom.*

"Yes?" The feminine voice through the intercom sounded bored.

"Scarlett Ashford." Thankfully she sounded calm and collected. "I've an appointment with Jackson Grayson at two."

The door clicked open and she stepped inside. The

reception area was small and minimalist, with a couple of hard backed chairs for clients. Clearly not designed to impress, or for comfort.

A girl with pink spiky hair and a nose ring sat on the edge of a desk and raked her gaze over Scarlett as though she were making up her mind whether or not to throw her back out on the street. On the wall behind the desk was a massive glossy poster of a white Bengal tiger. Across the top of the poster ran the legend:

Humans Suck Ass.

For a second, Scarlett was tempted to turn around and forget the whole thing. Except, her other options were pretty much zero.

"Take a seat." The pixie slid off the desk and pursed her jet-black lips in disapproval. The girl strutted across the floor toward the middle door at the back of the reception and, without knocking, opened it just enough to stick her head inside. "Scarlett Ashford is here for you, J."

She didn't hear any response but clearly Jackson Grayson made one, as the girl turned around and gestured her forward, opening the door for her.

Scarlett stood, and then forgot how to breathe.

The man before her, taking up more space than any mortal had any right to, was over six feet tall, with muscles filling out his black tee to the point of indecency.

He looks like Thor.

Her mouth dried as she dragged her fascinated gaze up from his biceps. *Don't think about his biceps.* She focused on his stubble-darkened jaw instead, but that didn't help. She'd never gone for the unshaven look before, but to hell with that.

Stop staring at him.

Good advice. A shame she couldn't follow it.

The gossip at work hadn't done him justice. He was so right for her purposes it was unnerving.

"I'll leave you to it then," the girl said. Scarlett had completely forgotten about her. She tried to ignore Jackson's messy black hair, which brushed his collar. And failed.

Thor's body. Loki's hair. Could it get any better?

"Yeah. Thanks, Ella."

Yes, it could. Even his voice dripped with sin. Dark and dangerous with a hint of deadly menace. Darts of pleasure stirred in places she'd almost forgotten she had.

How was that even possible? They hadn't even touched, and she was more turned on than she'd been in ages.

The click of the shutting door cut through her lustful thoughts.

Pull yourself together. She was here on business. Jackson Grayson would never take her seriously if all she could do was drool over him.

She slipped on the coolly polite mask she'd perfected in boarding school and stepped toward him. "Scarlett Ashford."

His hand enveloped hers. His grip was firm but the way his fingers brushed the back of hers was oddly intimate. He didn't appear to be in any hurry to break contact.

"Jackson Grayson."

Up close and personal it was hard to breathe. His face was rugged perfection. *Just like his body.*

She pulled her hand free with as much dignity as she could.

Who gets wet just by touching a guy's hand?

You do.

She wanted to hire him for a specific job, not to share her bed.

Are you sure?

. . .

Jackson folded his arms and leaned his butt against his desk. Although he'd run his own internet search on Scarlett Ashford before their appointment, it hadn't prepared him for the reality.

Scarlett Ashford was fucking hot.

Her black shirt with matching pants and jacket weren't especially sexy but she could probably wear a garbage bag and look good enough to eat.

"Thank you for seeing me at such short notice."

Her voice was like honey—golden and rich.

"My pleasure." It certainly was. After the shitty week he'd had, just looking at her was enough to lift his mood. Her glossy blonde hair fell in soft waves to below her shoulders, her skin was flawless, and her blue eyes gave her a strange sense of innocence.

An illusion. No one associated with the Ashford media and communications empire was innocent.

He pushed himself off the edge of his desk and waited until Scarlett took the chair he offered her before he sat down.

"You told Ella we'd been recommended to you. By who?"

"I'd prefer not to say."

It had to have been a previous client. And no client would recommend a service they'd been unhappy with, so why did she feel the need to keep her source confidential?

He didn't need another client, especially one who refused to answer the most basic questions. If she was being difficult now, the chances were she'd be a nightmare.

He should tell her he wasn't interested. Except... he couldn't.

You're going to regret this.

She brushed nonexistent dust from her thigh before taking a deep breath that caused her breasts to strain against the silky material of her shirt. It took him a couple of seconds to drag his gaze back to her face. *She's a potential client.* He didn't hit on clients, no matter how hot they were.

"Mr. Grayson."

"Call me Jackson."

The tip of her tongue slid along her lips. He couldn't work out whether she did it on purpose to distract him, or because she was nervous.

She didn't look nervous.

"Jackson." She inclined her head as though she were a queen. Then again, she was a princess in the world she lived in. "I want to hire your services for twelve hours next Saturday."

It was an emergency job. She'd told Ella that on the phone the other day when she made the appointment. Not only had she declined to say who had recommended them, she'd refused to explain what the job entailed. This had not endeared her to Ella, who'd researched her online and discovered the twenty-four-year-old Scarlett was a trust fund baby whose father was getting remarried next Saturday.

Next Saturday. Jackson frowned. "Is this connected to your father's wedding?"

If she was surprised by his remark she didn't show it.

"Yes. I need you to accompany me to the wedding and reception. People would need to think that we're a couple."

A time waster. So why was he still interested?

"One problem with that, *Scarlett*." He used her name even through she hadn't invited him to. "I don't run an escort agency."

A delicate blush heated her cheeks. Anyone would think he'd just offended her. He should've been pissed at her, but he wasn't.

Why would a woman like Scarlett Ashford want to hire a man for the night?

She could have any man she wanted.

"You misunderstand me." The hint of huskiness in her tone did nothing to stop the graphic fantasies invading his perverted mind. "I don't want to hire you for sex. I need a bodyguard."

Jackson forced himself to lean back in his chair. He'd thrown the escort agency line at her to get under her skin. He hadn't expected her to toss it back in his face like that. He wasn't sure it was a good thing that her answer hooked his interest more than ever.

"Why not use one of your own personal bodyguards?"

"No one would believe we were dating. Fraternization is cause for instant dismissal."

He laughed. She sounded so fucking prim and proper.

"And you expect me to believe you can't find a date for your own father's wedding?"

"Of course I can find a date. But I don't want a date. I want *you*."

Her last word thudded in the air between them.

I need to end this now. Scarlett Ashford was trouble.

"You want me, huh?" He gave a mocking smile so she wouldn't guess how much he wanted her to say "*yes*."

"Purely business, of course." She cleared her throat and brushed another speck of imaginary dirt from her black pants. "There's a reason why I need someone who looks as though they won't take any crap from anyone. It's… personal."

"You mean you want a bit of rough on your arm."

She frowned. "No, that isn't what I meant. I need someone…" Her voice trailed away. Her gaze lingered on his biceps and chest. He had the strangest conviction she didn't even realize what she was doing. Finally she finished checking him out. "Someone who won't be intimidated by my family."

No chance a bunch of entitled assholes could intimidate him. And then a possible reason for her odd request occurred to him.

"Has someone in your family threatened you?" Why else would she hire a complete stranger to pose as her date?

She sighed. "It's nothing so melodramatic. I just need certain… *people* to know that I'm not available."

Now he got it. She wanted to warn off an ex-lover who refused to take no for an answer.

He could do that. In fact, he was looking forward to it. Not that he was going to let Scarlett Ashford know that yet. She had secrets, and he didn't like being kept in the dark.

"If I accept this assignment, what are the boundaries of our relationship?"

It was obvious she didn't know whether to take issue with his use of *boundaries* or *relationship* first.

"I'm not sure I quite understand your meaning." She fixed a polite smile on her face.

He folded his arms on his desk and leaned toward her. He was enjoying this, probably more than he should, given that Scarlett was soon going to be his client.

"I don't want to cross any line." Not that he'd mind but he didn't want her to give him a bad Yelp review. "So I need to know in advance how physical you want us to be in public."

The tip of her tongue peeked between her lips again, for one tempting second. "Physical?"

"Yeah. I take it holding hands is okay. What about wrapping my arm around your waist when we dance?"

"Uh." Scarlett looked as if he'd just sucker-punched her. "I guess that would be acceptable."

"And kissing? Will that be cheek contact only, a brief touch of the lips, or major tongue penetration?"

Grayson 1, Ashford 0.

"Major tongue penetration might be required. Does your standard fee cover it, or would that incur hazard pay?"

He gave her a slow grin, not bothering to hide his interest. She'd thrown down the gauntlet.

Grayson 1, Ashford 1.

"I'll give you a special rate."

She didn't even flinch, and his respect for her went up a notch. "Does that mean you accept the job?"

He liked that she hadn't assumed anything. Given her background, he wouldn't have been surprised if she thought she was doing him a favor by wanting to hire his services.

"We need to fill out some paperwork, but yeah." He'd let her keep her secrets, if they meant so much to her. But when it came to the financial side of things, he never left anything to chance.

Twenty minutes later he saw Scarlett off the premises and to her car. As he watched her drive away, he realized Ella was by his side in the doorway.

He slammed the door shut. He hoped she hadn't seen the grin on his face.

"Put your tongue away, J." Ella gave a snort of laughter. "You're drooling."

"I don't drool over clients."

"So you're going to do whatever it is she wants? Why am I not surprised?"

Jackson sighed. He and his brothers had grown up next door to Ella and her family. She was the little sister they'd never had, and the obvious choice to join them five years ago when they'd set up their bodyguard and security business.

Her street smarts and take no prisoners attitude had quickly evolved into a sharp business brain. She kept the Grayson brothers' shit straight, and they'd be lost without her.

And she knew it.

"The money's good, and I'll be rubbing shoulders with the rich and famous."

Ella narrowed her eyes. "You don't need the money, and you despise the rich and famous. There's only one reason why you're taking this job."

"And why's that?" He towered over her but she didn't back down. Ella never backed down.

She smiled up at him, deceptively sweet. "Don't forget the Graysons's cardinal rule, honey. Never fuck clients."

Chapter Two

The wedding service was interminable. Scarlett tried to keep her focus on her father and Clarissa as they exchanged vows but it was impossible when Jackson Grayson's presence overshadowed everything.

Until the moment she'd seen him walk onto the grounds of the hotel her father had hired for the weekend's festivities, she hadn't been absolutely sure he'd show.

She flexed her fingers under cover of her oversized flower arrangement. At least she wasn't the chief maid of honor and responsible for holding the ridiculously huge bridal bouquet as well. Considering this was her father's third marriage and Clarissa's second, Scarlett couldn't help feeling everything about this wedding was way too over the top. From the eight bridesmaids to the six flower girls and four cute little ring bearers, everyone and every accessory complemented the not-so-blushing bride.

Everything was just exactly as Clarissa had demanded it.

Everything except for one minor detail: Scarlett, her malleable soon-to-be stepdaughter, had dared to turn down the partner Clarissa had procured for her. The man she had assured Scarlett's father—a week before she'd deigned to tell Scarlett her plans—would be the perfect match for his only daughter.

A bridesmaid without a suitable partner would upset Clarissa's demand for pleasing symmetry. And clearly she hadn't trusted Scarlett to come up with the necessary goods before the big day.

Surreptitiously, she looked over to where Jackson sat behind her immediate family. He caught her glance and gave that slow, sexy smile.

Whoa. Smolder alert. Heat prickled across her skin and it was suddenly hard to breathe.

In a formal suit and blindingly white shirt, he radiated a primitive aura of raw sex and dangerous, don't-fuck-with-me attitude. Exactly what she wanted. There was no way Clarissa's slimy cousin would hit on her with Jackson by her side.

She couldn't stop staring at him. The other bridesmaids, all from Clarissa's side of the family, had begun checking him out as soon as they caught sight of him.

She bit back a smile.

He's mine.

At least for the night.

Finally the formalities were over. A marquee had been set up by the river, and the early June weather was behaving perfectly for Clarissa. As the bridal party started to stroll toward the marquee, Clarissa's younger sister, who was only a few years older than Scarlett, fluttered her hand in front of her face in a dramatic fashion.

"Who's the guy in the seventh row? Ever seen him before? Hey, Scarlett, is he a long lost cousin or something?"

Before Scarlett could answer, another woman chimed in. "I don't care who he is. Look out ladies, because tonight that man is mine."

The hell he was. Scarlett had paid top dollar for Jackson's time and she had no intention of sharing him with anyone. Especially not anyone related by blood to Clarissa.

For the rest of the night, as far as everyone was concerned, she and Jackson were a couple. It didn't matter that she would never see him again. No one else knew that. Clarissa wouldn't care who she was dating once the wedding was over. She'd only insisted on pairing up Scarlett with her cousin Edward Saunders so the wedding footage and photos were perfect and well balanced.

The deluded Edward didn't get that she had no interest in him.

It would have been easier to go along with Clarissa's wishes and let Edward have his moment of fantasy. For the sake of peace, and to save her father any unnecessary stress, she had almost caved. But that overheard phone call had been the last straw.

She was nobody's bitch, least of all her new stepmother's.

With what she hoped was a mysterious smile, she broke ranks with the other attendants and went over to Jackson. Behind her, she heard a collective gasp of disbelief from the bridesmaids. Scarlett Ashford never put a foot out of place in public, and she certainly didn't get cozy with guys like Jackson.

"Hi, honey," she said, in case any of the guests were listening. She leaned toward him, intending to give him a quick kiss before returning to the bridal party. But Jackson gave her a wicked grin, grabbed her hand, and pulled her onto his lap.

"You look good enough to eat, babe." His low growl sent shivers racing over her bare arms and along the back of her neck.

She didn't have to wonder if anyone was eavesdropping. Everyone appeared to be *watching*.

Scarlett avoided the media circus that so many of her relatives thrived on, preferring to live a quieter existence. But this little demonstration was necessary.

A giggle bubbled in her chest. At least she didn't have to worry about being splashed across the gossip pages. The paparazzi had been banned from attending the wedding, and the security was watertight.

"So do you," she whispered.

His thumb stroked the back of her hand. He probably didn't even realize he was doing it.

"You smell wonderful." His hot breath tickled her ear and she shifted on his lap.

Damn, that felt good.

"You smell pretty good yourself." She traced her finger over his shoulder. "Scrub up well, don't you?"

All she wanted to do was close her eyes and relish the feel of his rigid muscles as they enveloped her. Another couple of seconds wouldn't matter.

She felt him smile against the soft skin below her ear. "I may be wearing a suit, but just so you know, I've still gone commando."

• • •

Scarlett tensed and hastily pulled herself upright. Her pupils were huge, her lips parted, and for one crazy second he thought she was going to kiss him. She took a deep breath, and her glossy pink lips curved into the sexiest smile he'd ever seen.

"I should hope you are." Her voice was low, with a hint of huskiness that arrowed straight to his dick.

He should have known Scarlett would come back with a comment that was guaranteed to turn up the heat.

Much as he wanted to continue this conversation—hell, it was more than conversation he wanted to continue with her—she'd hired him for the specific purpose of showing people she wasn't available. Since she appeared to be in no immediate danger of harassment from any ex-lover, and a good portion of the guests now knew Scarlett was with him, he released her hand.

"I'll see you back at the tent." He couldn't help grinning when she shook her head at him in mock despair before she turned and caught up with the others.

Her slinky green dress fell to just above her ankles and molded to her waist and ass as though she'd been poured into it. Her hair was a mass of curls piled on top of her head, threaded through with more of the flowers she had in her bouquet.

He imagined pulling out those flowers one by one, and then spearing his fingers through her hair until her blonde curls tumbled around her shoulders.

Why was he torturing himself? Scarlett Ashford was a client. And clients were off limits.

The tie was suffocating him. He tugged it loose and undid the top button of his shirt. He scanned the interior of the marquee for about the sixth time since the speeches had started.

This was Scarlett's world. Moneyed and privileged. While he'd grown up on the back streets, literally fighting for survival.

As the final speaker sat down, and waiters appeared as if by magic, his gaze once again returned to Scarlett. She was at the top table along with the rest of the bridal party, and the guy next to her needed to back the fuck off. Scarlett was angled away from him but it didn't appear to deter the little shit. As Jackson watched, the guy took Scarlett's hand and pulled it beneath the table.

Fuck that. It might be innocent or he might be rubbing her hand along his dick. He pushed his chair back and made his way toward her. Heads turned and watched his progress. Obviously marching toward the top table wasn't done at high society weddings but as far as he was concerned, neither was hitting on a woman when she wasn't interested.

He reached the table and planted his hands on the pristine white cloth. Scarlett blinked up at him as though she couldn't believe her eyes. He turned to the guy next to her. He looked about thirty, and he stared at Jackson as though he was shit on his shoe.

"Hey, babe," Jackson drawled, returning his attention to Scarlett. "I'm missing you already. Thought I'd take you back with me."

"Scarlett?" The guy turned to her. "Do you know this… person?"

Jackson watched Scarlett tug her hand free. "Of course

I do, Edward." She sounded breathless. "This is Jackson. My date."

Jackson couldn't stop himself. He leaned over the table so only she and the prick could hear. "My lover."

He wasn't sure if he was crossing the line. He didn't care. She wanted someone who didn't give a shit about causing offense. He was her man.

"Come on." He took Scarlett's hand. "You're joining me at my table."

Chapter Three

Scarlett clutched Jackson's hand as he led her through the marquee, after practically dragging her from the top table. He hadn't even asked her, just assumed she was fine with it.

Not that she exactly objected to his high-handed behavior and, if she was honest, she found it fun. Except for the fact that, again, she was the focus of attention.

"Was that your ex?"

In the four-inch heels Clarissa had insisted her bridesmaids wear, she stood five-foot-eight. Yet Jackson still towered over her like some kind of mythical warrior, sworn to protect her.

I really shouldn't enjoy that visual so much. It was pretty barbaric.

"Edward isn't my ex. He's Clarissa's cousin. She thought we would make a lovely couple."

Was it her imagination or did Jackson's jaw tighten in disapproval?

"Don't worry about him. He'll soon get the message you're not available."

Her good mood deflated. Jackson had simply been doing his job. The job she'd hired him for. How had she forgotten that, for even a few fleeting seconds?

"He knows I'm not available." She tried to keep the acid from her voice but wasn't sure she succeeded. "He just won't take no for an answer."

Jackson stopped by a table near the back of the marquee and pulled her tight against his side. He bent his head until his jaw grazed her cheek.

Oh God, yes. His stubble was even better than she'd imagined.

"I can have a chat with him if you want. Make him see the error of his ways."

It took Scarlett a moment to realize his husky whisper masked a serious threat. Or was he joking? She frowned up into his face.

He wasn't joking.

"Violence isn't the answer." She saw the result of that every time she went to work. "Edward's a jerk, that's all."

"What makes you think I'd be violent with him?"

Although he didn't raise his voice, she heard the tense undercurrent in his words, as though her remark had hit a nerve.

She hadn't meant to offend him. She sighed and went onto her toes so she was closer to his ear.

"I'm sorry. I guess it's because I often want to knee him in the nuts, so I assume everyone else wants to as well."

"Sure."

He didn't sound mad, so why did she still have the feeling

that she'd inadvertently crossed an invisible line?

"Hey." Jackson caught the attention of a passing waiter. Not that it was hard, since most of the staff and half the guests at this end of the marquee apparently could not tear their scandalized gazes away from him. "Can you bring another chair and place setting?"

"Right away, sir." The waiter darted off, clearly more in awe of Jackson than afraid of Clarissa's fury at having her table settings disrupted. Still holding her around her waist, Jackson turned to the enthralled guests at his table.

"Mind shoving round so there's room for Scarlett?" It was phrased as a question but everyone knew it wasn't.

Once they were seated, Jackson draped his arm around her shoulder. He took his bodyguard duties seriously. She tried not to let that thought spoil the mood. Leaning against Jackson and feeling his fingers idly caress her naked shoulder more than made up for Edward's attempted mauling during the photo shoot.

"How long have you two been seeing each other?" Zahara, who Scarlett knew was a big deal behind the scenes in the music industry, asked.

"A while," Scarlett said.

"Long enough," Jackson said at the same moment. The grin he shot her caused all sorts of warm fluttery sensations between her thighs.

"Haven't seen you around before. Are you part of the Ashford empire?" Scarlett didn't recognize the guy who spoke but she recognized his type—a sycophant, sniffing out potential new blood.

"No." Jackson threaded his fingers through one of her torturously created curls before focusing his attention on the other man. "I run a dojo on Heyward Street."

Scarlett managed to hide her surprise by picking up her wine glass and taking a sip. Heyward Street was maybe ten minutes away from the Graysons' office, in an equally run down area of town.

She was grateful he didn't tell the truth. That kind of gossip was great fodder for the tabloids.

The man grunted and sat back, obviously no longer interested in worming his way into Jackson's good opinion, since he wasn't in a position of power in the Ashford empire.

"Heyward Street?" Zahara tapped her sunburst-decorated fingernail against her matching lips. "Isn't that area in the middle of a redevelopment?"

"That's right." Jackson's fingers played along her nape. It was seriously distracting. "We're behind the petition to keep the vultures out of the neighborhood."

"Fascinating," Zahara said.

"That's one way of looking at it." Jackson didn't raise his voice, but tension radiated from him. It was obvious he was dead set against the redevelopment, and while she privately agreed with him, she didn't want to get into a heated discussion about it right now.

If Zahara or any of the others persisted with this line of conversation, Jackson wouldn't hesitate to share his opinion. His total lack of ass-kissing was, after all, part of the reason she'd hired him.

Except she'd only wanted him to pretend in front of Edward and any interfering members of her extended family, not associates and acquaintances of her father. She had the feeling Jackson wouldn't care about her lines in the sand, even if she'd thought to share them with him.

The best plan of action was to get Jackson outside before he said anything else.

"I need some fresh air. Are you coming, honey?"

He turned toward her. The beginning of a smile quirked his lips and there was a wicked gleam in his eyes. He leaned in close, under pretext of helping her to her feet.

"After you, Scarlett." His whisper might have been completely innocent but she doubted it, considering the way his eyes locked with hers and his thumb brushed over her hand. Her cheeks warmed and she bit her lip to stop herself from laughing. She didn't dare glance at anyone at the table, in case someone had overheard him and possessed a mind as filthy as her own.

They escaped through the back exit. The dinner and speeches had gone on forever, and the sun was low in the sky, casting a magical twilight glow across the river. It was the perfect romantic spot. What a pity Jackson wasn't really her date.

"Thanks, Jackson." She kicked off her high-heeled sandals and curled her toes in the grass. Bliss. The damn things had been killing her all day.

"What for?" His smoky voice tugged her back to the present. She had to crane her neck to look him in the eye.

For an eternal moment she forgot why she had thanked him.

"Oh." She cleared her throat. It didn't do a lot to clear her head. "For your quick thinking back there, about running a dojo."

"I do run a dojo."

That hadn't come up in the brief internet search she'd done on *Graysons'*.

"And you're behind the petition to stop the redevelopment?" At least she'd heard of that, mainly because Edward was involved on the other side of the fence and had complained bitterly at the last family lunch that the *ignorant masses*—his words—stalling the planning permission were gaining traction.

"Sure am. Those kids need somewhere to go, besides the gutter."

Did he know who Edward was? It would account for the look Jackson had shot him when he'd reached the top table. She'd imagined it was because he hadn't liked the way Edward had been pawing her, but realistically how likely was that?

Edward was the last person she wanted to think about right now, let alone talk about with Jackson. She'd much rather talk about *him*.

"So you're a philanthropist. Bit of a dark horse, aren't you?"

"I've never been called a philanthropist before. But I'll take it."

She laughed, and when he grinned back her knees all but gave way. "So why a dojo?"

He slid his fingers through hers and pulled her toward him. *He's only doing it for show.* But it didn't make any difference. A million tiny tremors raced along her arm.

"Why not?" His sinfully seductive voice wove through her senses and it took her a couple of seconds to realize that he hadn't answered her question. That he obviously didn't *want* to answer her question.

I don't care. Except the truth was, she did. Crazy, since this wasn't a real date.

You're his client.

It was like a wet slap across her face.

She flattened her palm against his chest, just in case anyone caught sight of them.

Admit it. You just want to touch him.

Jackson clearly had no objection to them getting physical, so she might as well enjoy it while she could.

"I think my plan worked. If he thinks I'm going out with you, Edward won't bother me any more."

The lazy smile on Jackson's face vanished. "I don't know why you didn't just tell him to go screw himself."

"I've done everything but." When she realized she was stroking Jackson's chest, she forced herself to stop. "He's oblivious. Seriously, he belongs in the nineteenth century. As far as he's concerned no woman is complete without a man in her life. And being without a man is definitely not something she'd choose to do willingly."

"Then you should've kneed him in the nuts like you wanted to. Trust me, he'd get the message loud and clear."

There was no way she'd ever resort to physical violence, but the grim expression on Jackson's face, combined with the mental image of Edward clutching his valuables, was too funny, and she giggled. Jackson tugged her closer. It was dangerously intoxicating.

"Clarissa would definitely have had something to say about that."

"So what?" He frowned. It was obvious he couldn't see the problem. Then again, he didn't know Clarissa.

Scarlett had the overpowering urge to confide in him, but he wouldn't care about her personal troubles.

With a sense of disbelief, she realized she was once again

stroking his chest. He'd think she was totally depraved. The problem was, she couldn't seem to stop herself.

"It's not Clarissa I care about upsetting. She has my dad wrapped around her little finger and he just wants rainbows and unicorns for her." It was a little annoying the way her father indulged every tiny whim of Clarissa's. "What I mean is, she'd complain to him if I assaulted her precious cousin. I wouldn't want to cause Dad any upset."

Jackson was still frowning. "You're too nice."

She guessed he meant it as a compliment. But something about it scraped along her nerves. Because she was sure Jackson Grayson didn't date *nice girls*.

Where the hell did that come from? "It's got nothing to do with being nice." She hoped the waspish tone was all in her head. Jackson didn't deserve to be on the receiving end of her pique. "It's because my dad... he's not very well. I won't be responsible for putting him under any additional stress."

Jackson grunted. Scarlett stared at him, her irritation forgotten. He was genuinely pissed...on her behalf.

"*Edward*," he said the name as though it offended him, "sounds like an abusive asshole."

It was on the tip of her tongue to automatically defend Edward but the words lodged in her throat.

Her own grandmother had suffered years of emotional abuse from her husband. Scarlett's mom had set up a women's shelter in her memory, and Scarlett volunteered there. She was aware of the warning signs. But she had completely missed the red flags with Edward, instead making excuses for his possessiveness and unwarranted groping.

Then again, she wasn't in a relationship with Edward.

Even so, the fact that it had taken a virtual stranger to point his dangerous behavior out to her wasn't exactly comfortable.

Jackson stared at her. His frown was gone and the smile he aimed her way drove every sane thought from her head.

"The dancing has started," he said.

Chapter Four

Scarlett blinked in apparent surprise. "You want to dance?"

Dancing was optional. *I just want you in my arms.* And, he had to be honest, to show that prick Edward Saunders she most definitely was off limits.

He had to stop thinking about that jerk. It wasn't as though Scarlett had ever been out with him. But his kind pushed his buttons — a fucking dickwad who thought a woman's only function was to service his needs.

He'd seen enough of that type in his life. His own father had been one of the worst offenders.

With a suppressed shudder, he shoved the image of his father from his mind. Bastard was long dead, and thank God for that. He pulled his focus back to Scarlett.

"Dancing was part of the deal, remember?" He grinned when a frown creased her forehead. It appeared she wasn't thrilled with the reminder that she'd hired him, although he couldn't figure out why that pleased him. "Plus we haven't explored the major tongue penetration yet. I always aim to give full satisfaction in all areas."

Scarlett made a strange noise, as though she was choking. But then she let out a long breath and shook her head. Her curls bounced around her face.

"Don't worry. I'll let you know if I'm not… fully satisfied." Her last words were breathless, and a sexy blush heated her cheeks.

His cock stirred. Shit.

She's a client.

And as Ella had so kindly pointed out, he did not fuck clients.

But she was only a client for another eight hours.

Scarlett pushed her feet into the wickedly high heels she'd kicked off. He had the feeling he was becoming obsessed with the idea of having her. Was it because he knew the chances of her agreeing to a quick fuck were next to zero?

She might have hired him to be her fake date. She might be willing to make out in public. But there was something about her that told him she wasn't the type to have a one-night stand.

Scarlett was a commitment kind of girl. And commitment wasn't in his vocabulary.

She bent over to fiddle with the delicate straps on her shoes and he couldn't tear his gaze away from her ass. The slinky material of her dress clung like a second skin. Was she wearing anything underneath? Sure as hell didn't look like it.

He wished she'd forget about her shoes and stand up. The temptation to run his palms over her butt was powerful.

It took a considerable amount of self-restraint to keep his hands to himself.

They were in public, and for fuck's sake, he wasn't a horny teen. Oh, and he was on the job.

Yeah. *If only she wasn't so...*

Maybe Scarlett wasn't into commitment as much as he imagined.

Finally, she stood up and wobbled. "Damn shoes." She glanced over her bare shoulder at him. "Have you changed your mind?"

He was still enjoying the view. "I don't change my mind." He led her back into the marquee. An orchestra was playing, and the bride and Scarlett's father were waltzing around the dance floor. Yeah, wouldn't catch him doing any waltzing. When he danced with a woman it was all up close and personal.

He glanced at Scarlett. She was watching her father with a brooding expression. She obviously had issues, and he was willing to bet it was more than just not wanting to upset him because of his ill health.

Good thing she hadn't hired him to sort that out. He was no good with issues that involved parents. The nearest he'd had to a father figure growing up had been his older brother Alex. And look how that had turned out.

He shoved the memories aside. Shoved the guilt aside. Alex was doing great now. More than great. He was, after all, the driving force behind the whole concept of *Graysons'*.

A few other couples strolled onto the dance floor. He wound his arm around Scarlett's waist.

"Don't expect me to do any fancy stuff," he warned her.

She linked her hands behind his neck but didn't press

her body against his. Probably just as well. He wasn't sure he wanted her to feel just how hard he was. It was one thing to flirt and mess around. It was another if she realized he wasn't doing it simply because she was paying him.

It had nothing to do with the fact he was still under contract.

He'd shred that contract as soon as he got back to the office.

"Fancy stuff?" There was a faintly mocking note in her voice. "Like *Dirty Dancing* you mean?"

He slid his hands over the curve of her hips. It didn't help his resolve to keep things purely professional between them.

His jaw grazed the soft skin of her cheek. "I can do dirty." He breathed the words against her ear. "I just don't do the dancing."

So much for keeping it professional.

She edged a little closer. Without his meaning to, his hands slipped and he cupped her ass. Lust spiked through his groin. God, that was the wrong move to make. She fit him perfectly. With a silent curse he molded her waist instead.

"I can do the dancing." Scarlett's whisper was husky. "Looks like we're evenly matched, Jackson."

He tried not to think about all the dirty things he'd like to do to her. With a primitive growl, he tugged her tight against his body. She gasped, whether at the way he held her or because she could feel his dick digging into her, he wasn't sure.

"You want to test that theory further?"

What the hell was he doing? He didn't want to start rumors that he did escort work. His brothers would kill him if they found out he'd slept with a client.

Eight more hours. *They'd never find out…*

Scarlett's fingers stilled in his hair. Her glossy lips parted. It appeared he wasn't the only one having trouble dragging air into his lungs.

"I might." Her whisper was breathless, and for a second he didn't have a clue what she was talking about. "What do you have in mind, theoretically?"

Was she serious? Or just continuing their game of fake flirtation? But if she wasn't playing, he needed to set the ground rules from the start. "Theoretically." He drifted his lips across her soft hair. Whatever shampoo she used drove him wild. "For a no holds barred one-night stand?"

"Yes." Her voice was so low he didn't hear the sound, just watched her lips form the word.

It was only a theoretical yes. It didn't mean she was going to wrap her legs around him. Except the way she looked at him, and the way her fingers tightened in his hair, told him something different.

Thank fuck for that.

He wrapped his hand around the back of her neck. Her curls teased his knuckles. He leaned toward her until their foreheads touched and their breath mingled.

"I'll take you down to the river."

"How would you take me?" Her whisper cut across his fantasy, but in the best possible way. "Would you carry me?"

He liked the way her mind worked. "Over my shoulder."

"Neanderthal."

"Then I'd strip you naked." He thought of something. "Except for your heels."

Her fingernails trailed along his nape. It pushed his

control dangerously near the edge.

"You like my heels?"

"I like you wearing the heels." There was a difference.

"What about you? Would you be naked too?"

"Down by the river? No way."

She pouted. Her lips begged to be kissed. He wasn't sure how much longer he could hold off tasting them.

"That hardly seems fair." Her voice was all kinds of husky. "You'd be having all the fun."

He brushed his lips across hers. Her breath caught, and he lingered, savoring the feather light touch.

"Babe, you'd have plenty of fun. Trust me, you have no idea what I can do with my mouth."

For a moment he didn't think she was going to answer. Then the tip of her tongue slid over her lips, as though she was tasting the words, assessing his challenge.

And then she spoke.

"I wouldn't mind finding out."

Chapter Five

What the hell had she just said? The blood burned in her cheeks, but she couldn't tear her gaze away from Jackson. He gave her a smile so full of wicked intent, she had no idea how her legs managed to keep her upright.

She had just agreed to have sex with Jackson Grayson. A one-night stand, no less, something she'd never done.

No way was she going to back out of it. For tonight, at least, she was done with being a *nice girl*. Tonight she was going to let her inner vixen escape and enjoy everything Jackson offered.

"You want to get out of here?"

The music faded into the background, and the other guests became strangely ghostlike. The erratic thud of her heart pounded in her ears.

He wanted her. Here and now.

Holy fuck.

"Sure." She hoped she sounded sultry and not as though

she was battling a flood of nerves. For a moment, the image of her hotel room flashed through her mind. They'd be comfortable and safe from unexpected discovery there. But tonight wasn't about being *comfortable* or *safe*. "The river, right?"

As he slowly maneuvered their swaying bodies around the other couples on the perimeter of the dance floor, his mouth brushed against her ear. "If we make it that far."

She clutched his shoulders for support. She'd never been so turned on by a guy's words before. Then again, no guy had ever spoken to her the way Jackson did.

Was he really going to follow through on his promise to strip her naked? *Outside*? As they left the marquee a shiver raced over her bare arms. She wasn't sure whether it was caused by anticipation or alarm.

"Cold?" Before she could tell Jackson she was so hot she might spontaneously combust, he shrugged off his jacket and draped it around her shoulders. "Better?"

She didn't need it, but his body heat enveloped her in a silken cocoon. She inhaled the subtle scent of his woodsy cologne.

"Much better." She hoped she sounded like a provocative siren. At least Jackson wouldn't guess she'd never done anything this daring before.

She hoped.

He pulled her close and she snuggled against his solid strength. She hoped to God he had a condom handy. The thought caused an exquisite ache to spiral through her, and she wound her arm around him. He was so big.

Was he that big all over?

Tiny fairy lights had been strung through the branches of the majestic jacarandas, illuminating the purple blooms in a magical, fluorescent canopy of lace. In the distance, the river glinted, and nerves danced in the pit of her stomach.

He really was heading in that direction.

Then he veered to the right, away from the river, where shadows beckoned in trees not draped in wedding finery. With every step away from the celebration inside the marquee, Scarlett's heart thudded harder against her ribs. In the silvery light of the moon she saw the predatory gleam in his eyes. It was dangerous and exhilarating.

Without warning, he swung her around and pinned her against a tree. She gasped and flattened her hands against his chest. "This wasn't part of the plan."

His hands cradled her face. "No, it wasn't."

"Second thoughts?" Her fingers dug into his rock hard pecs. Frantic denial fluttered through her. He couldn't change his mind. Not now.

She hadn't been with a guy in months. Was that why she wanted him so badly?

Or maybe it was just *him*.

"No second thoughts."

She let out a ragged breath. He didn't change his mind and he didn't have second thoughts. It might not be a great way to live your life, but it sure suited her for tonight.

"One more thing." His thumbs stroked her cheeks. The gesture was oddly tender. "None of this has got anything to do with the job you hired me to do. It's because I want you."

He moved closer. Her hands were squashed between their bodies and her back jammed up against the bark of the tree. The hard length of his erection burned through the silk of her dress, branding her.

He really was that big all over. "So…" She licked her lips.

What did she want to say? "Not the river, then?"

"I like it here just fine." His hands slid beneath his jacket and over her bare shoulders. "Ever fucked under a tree before?"

She'd only ever done it in bed. With the lights off. No way was she going to tell him *that*.

"Have you?" She finally managed to move her hands from between their bodies, and palmed his ass. *Commando*. If only his damn pants weren't in the way.

"Can't say I have." His hands cupped her breasts and she stifled a moan. "First time for everything I guess."

She writhed helplessly, and the flimsy thong she was wearing stretched tight over her sex. *That was so good.* But it wasn't enough.

"Jackson." *I need you.* She couldn't say it. His body tensed, as though hearing her say his name triggered a primitive reaction.

"Scarlett." It was a raw whisper, and then his mouth claimed hers.

He wasn't gentle or refined about it. His kiss was savage, punishing, and so fucking hot. She gripped his butt, forcing him closer. But it wasn't close enough.

It was dirty and wild and she loved every frenzied second of it. And then he pinched her nipples and she forgot how to think at all.

"Now." *Oh God, I'm begging.* "Please."

He panted in her face. *I did this to him.*

"You sure? I don't think I can stop once I'm inside you, so tell me now."

"I'm sure." For one brief moment, sanity hit her. "Do you have a condom?" She'd die if he didn't.

"Yeah." His voice was low and gravely and did nothing to cool the rabid need raging through her blood. He pulled out a packet from his pocket and ripped it open with his teeth.

Her hands slipped to his hips as he dragged open his fly. *This was really happening.* "Now."

"It's not going to be pretty." He speared his fingers through her hair and forced her to look at him. No one had ever grabbed her hair like that before. It was shockingly arousing. With his other hand he tugged her dress up her legs. "It's going to be hard and fast."

Her knees wobbled. Hard and fast sounded perfect.

"Good."

His fingers brushed against her swollen flesh, and in spite of the tree at her back she might have collapsed if Jackson wasn't still gripping her hair.

"You feel like silk." His husky words inflamed her as much as his touch. No man had ever talked to her like that.

A low moan escaped. She was so close to the edge. Didn't he know how badly she wanted him?

His lips brushed hers. "You're so fucking hot, Scarlett. Hot and wet. Do you want my cock inside you? Is that what you're waiting for?"

She clutched onto his shirt. Was he honestly waiting for an answer?

It appeared he was. She hitched in a shallow breath and found her voice. "Yes."

"Yes what?" He sounded feral, but still continued to torture her with teasing strokes and tantalizing dips into her wet cleft.

She licked her dry lips. She had never talked dirty in her life. But this was okay, because she was never going to see

Jackson again.

"I want your cock inside me, fucking me hard and fast."

She couldn't believe what she had just said. *Nice girls* didn't say those kinds of things. *One night stand. Sex under a tree.* Tonight was obviously going to be a trifecta of firsts.

Jackson shoved her thong aside. His eyes never left hers. Thrills chased through her at the riveted look on his face. He obviously found their conversation as electrifying as she did.

He shifted his angle and the head of his erection pushed into her. He was as big as she had imagined. She gripped his hips, pulling him closer, and his grin stole her breath.

"You want more?" His fingers teased her swollen lips, stretched wide by his penetration. She choked back a moan and flexed her internal muscles. Jackson let out a pained breath between his teeth.

"Give me everything." *Was that really her voice?* She sounded sexy and uninhibited. She could do or say anything and none of it would come back to taunt her in the morning. There would be no tomorrow with Jackson.

He rocked into her, filling her so completely she forgot how to breathe, how to think. His fingers tangled in her hair and she was crushed against the tree, immobile.

He filled her so completely. Erotic tremors rippled through her.

"You're so tight around me, Scarlett. I can't fucking breathe." His mouth crashed down on hers, his tongue claiming her as thoroughly as his cock. She bucked helplessly, and he teased her clit with the tip of one finger. Pleasure spiraled, and when he groaned it pushed her over the edge.

A frenzied, wild haze enveloped her. She clawed to get closer to him.

Jackson pounded into her, harder and faster. "Scarlett," he whispered against her lips as he came.

Their mouths clung together. After endless moments her mind surfaced from its cloud of bliss, the thud of her heart slowed and breathing eased.

And she remembered where they were.

At her father's wedding.

His fingers released their brutal grip on her hair and slowly he withdrew from her. She sucked in air as he made himself presentable, her palms pressed against the tree behind her. She wasn't sure she had the strength to stand unaided just yet.

Had anyone seen them? She risked a sideways glance, but the shadows revealed no one.

For a moment he stared at her. Her face heated, but she couldn't look away from him.

God, what happened now? Was she supposed to pull herself together, stroll back into the marquee with him, and act as though nothing had happened? Since they'd had sex would he consider his duties over for the night, and vanish?

Her inner vixen quailed at facing scores of wedding guests. She pressed her fingers against her bruised lips. Everyone would know what she'd been up to.

But she had no regrets. She had never been so *taken* before. Even the lingering memory was enough to cause exhausted quivers through her tender flesh. So mind-blowing orgasms didn't just happen in romance novels.

Ask him to come back to your room.

He tugged his jacket across her breasts and then lingered there, his knuckles pressing against her through the material. Desire stirred, licking through her blood.

Once just wasn't enough. She wanted to get naked with him, run her hands over him and explore his hard body at her leisure.

"You in a hurry to get back?" He nodded toward the distant marquee, but his gaze never left hers.

She licked her dry lips. "Not really."

"Your room or mine?"

He didn't have a room. Her father had booked them all. Jackson's room might be miles away.

"Mine."

"Sounds good." He slung his arm around her shoulders. She pulled back, slightly appalled he expected them to simply stroll into the hotel straight away. Suppose they bumped into her dad?

The last thing she wanted was for him to see her right after she'd had sex. That would give him another heart attack for sure.

"Jackson." She sounded mortified but couldn't help herself. "I need to…" Her voice trailed away as the truth hit her. Where exactly did she expect to freshen up? She had no intention of returning to the marquee, and there wasn't a bathroom located among the jacarandas.

"You need to what?" He appeared genuinely clueless. She knew it was dark, but couldn't he *see* what a mess she was?

"My *hair*." She was sure it looked like a bird's nest, considering Jackson had plunged his hand through it and rubbed it all over the tree.

"You look great." He pulled a lily from her hair and brushed the soft petals along her cheek. She wasn't sure she believed him, but relief tumbled through her all the same. "You look like you've just been fucked up against a tree."

Chapter Six

Jackson followed Scarlett into the elevator and hid his grin as the doors swished closed. She'd been ramrod straight in his arms as they walked to the hotel, and her regal acknowledgment of the receptionist's greeting hadn't hid her mortification.

It was obvious she had never been in this situation before. He wasn't sure why that amused him, but it did. And while anyone with half an eye could see they had just had a heavy make out session, he was damn sure no one would guess what had really gone down among the jacarandas.

It was equally clear Scarlett thought the entire world knew. Just because her hair was a bit messed up.

Okay, so he hadn't exactly said the right thing, but he hadn't expected her to take him seriously. He backed her into a corner of the elevator and planted his hands on the walls behind her shoulders. "No one saw us, babe."

"I know." Her hand fluttered up toward her head before

she stopped herself and folded her arms instead.

"No one knows I just fucked your brains out, either."

"Only because we didn't meet anyone on our way back here. I'm sure the guy at reception suspected something."

He resisted the urge to laugh. Generally, he believed high-maintenance girls were a pain in the ass, but Scarlett's fussiness was cute.

"The only reason he couldn't take his eyes off you is because you're the hottest woman at this wedding."

"Well, *hardly*." She gave a small smile, as though she didn't believe him. "At least *you* don't look as though you've been ravished by one of the bridesmaids."

"How do I look, then?"

She licked her lips. "Like the hottest guy at the wedding."

That's what she thought of him? "Is that right?" He couldn't help the grin. "You sure?"

"Stop fishing for compliments. We're here." She prodded his chest and, with reluctance, he backed off. Scarlett glanced up and down the hallway before she left the elevator.

"Should I check the fire escapes?"

"I'm sure this is hilarious for you, Jackson." She sighed and inserted the keycard into her door. "But I'm pretty sure we're safe now. Dad has the Presidential Suite on the top floor."

Her *dad*? She'd been worried about meeting her father?

He kicked the door shut and waited until Scarlett turned on the lights. For a second, the opulence of the suite distracted him. But only for a second.

He grabbed her hand and swung her around to face him. "I don't get it. You were fine with your dad and all the guests thinking we were lovers, before we'd done anything.

So what's the problem now?"

"But there's a difference between everyone thinking we're lovers and actually coming face-to-face with people right after… you know." A blush stained her cheeks. "That would be just…" She bit her lip. "Awkward."

For one crazy moment he was plunged back into his wild teenage years. After the illegally organized street fights he'd been involved in, there was always sex to be had in the surrounding abandoned buildings. Nobody cared who saw you, either during the act or afterwards.

Sure, he'd moved on from that lifestyle years ago, and he didn't miss either the fights or the fucking. But he had never given a shit if someone knew he'd just had sex.

He tugged on one of her curls and then wound the silky strands around his finger. *Awkward* wasn't the way he wanted her to remember their night together. *Fucking hot* was more like it. He was going to enjoy wiping every last negative thought from her head before morning.

Thank God he'd stuffed a pack of condoms in his pocket at the last moment. He almost hadn't bothered. Scarlett was off limits. But in the end his cock had ruled his head.

Just the way it had under the jacarandas.

"What are you smiling at?" Scarlett sounded defensive. Surely she didn't think he was laughing at her? He pulled her closer and feathered the tip of her curl across her full lips.

"The way this night is turning out. Got to be the best wedding I've ever attended."

"It's certainly a lot more fun than my dad's last wedding."

He really didn't want to discuss her father. But the comical distaste on Scarlett's face made him laugh. "No hot hook up to make the night bearable?"

She made a sound of disgust. He could feel the tension draining from her. "Hardly. I was eighteen and had just left boarding school. The deal was sealed on the family yacht in the Bahamas. They were divorced a year later."

Boarding school. The family yacht. Her world was so different from his that they might as well have been born on different planets. But tonight she was his, and their backgrounds didn't matter.

"How long do you give this one?" He led her into the sitting room. It was all muted gold and forest greens and was bigger than the ground floor of the house he and his brothers had grown up in.

"If Clarissa has her way it will be forever, and Dad is besotted by her, so who knows?" She shrugged and glanced at her shoulder, clearly surprised that she was still wearing his jacket. Just as well he'd given it to her when they left the marquee. Otherwise her back would've been scratched raw by the tree.

"True love, huh?" He took the jacket from her and tossed it over an elegant loveseat.

"I don't think so. His one true love died years ago. Cognac?" She made her way to the mini bar.

"Sure." He loosened his tie and dropped it on top of his jacket. Scarlett poured them both a generous measure of brandy before handing him a glass. He swirled the amber liquid and inhaled its rich, fruity aroma.

"Here's to us." Scarlett clinked glasses. "For one night only."

"I'll drink to that."

She threaded her fingers through his. He'd never noticed

before how the touch of a palm against his could be so arousing. "So, is there anyone special in your life, Jackson?"

He wasn't sure he wanted to get so personal with Scarlett, but her question bugged him. "Do you think I'd be here with you now if there was?"

"Oh." Scarlett raised her eyebrows. "Good answer."

"Just so you know, I haven't done this before."

She looked enthralled. It wasn't exactly the response he'd been looking for. "Shouldn't that be my line?"

"I'm not talking about one-night stands." He'd had plenty of those.

"I know what you're talking about. And I didn't mean to offend you. I'm sure you'd never be unfaithful if you were in a relationship."

For a second he was speechless. How had they gotten onto the subject of relationships and being faithful? The truth was, he'd never been in a proper relationship before. Didn't believe in them. He had the feeling if he told Scarlett that she would be less than impressed.

Not that he wanted to impress her. But why go out of his way to disillusion her about his nonexistent good qualities?

"You didn't offend me."

"Good."

Since she'd brought the subject up, he decided to satisfy his own curiosity. "What about you? Aside from that asshole Edward, is there any other man in your life?"

Just because she'd hired him to accompany her to this wedding, didn't necessarily mean she wasn't seeing someone on the quiet. Although he doubted it. Despite tonight, she still struck him as a commitment kind of girl.

"First of all, Edward isn't in my life in that way, even

if that would make my dad's day." She gave an impatient sigh and shook her head, as though she wanted to dislodge that thought. "And secondly, no I'm not seeing anyone else. I told you I was single. You don't seem like the type to think a woman's not whole without a man in her life."

He remembered she'd said that was Edward's view of the world. The possibility she had just likened him to that prick stung. Even if it was his own fault.

"I'm just surprised a beautiful woman like you is single. That's all."

Scarlett didn't appear thrilled by his attempt at flattery. He really needed to practice if he was going to make a habit of it. But until tonight he'd never even attempted flattery.

He took a long swallow of his cognac before he dug himself any deeper into the hole.

"If you must know I haven't been in a relationship for over five months."

He had no idea what to say in response to that. When he hooked up with a woman he wasn't interested in her previous sexploits. Except this time he'd asked Scarlett. And he hadn't just asked her. He actively wanted to know.

What the fuck was that all about?

Chapter Seven

It appeared Jackson had no intention of responding. Scarlett had always thought discussing personal details was off limits when indulging in a one-night stand, but it hadn't stopped Jackson from asking about her love life. And she was pretty sure he was experienced when it came to this kind of situation.

Within three seconds, she couldn't stand her curiosity any longer. "So how long has it been since you've been in a relationship?"

He sent her a smoldering look. Did he practice those sizzling glances or did they just come naturally? Her nipples chafed against her dress and she took a sip of brandy before she started drooling.

"I don't do relationships."

Somehow that wasn't a surprise. The pang of regret that speared through her chest, however, was.

Get a grip. She didn't care if Jackson was a commitment-phobe. *We're not dating.*

"What do you do, then?" The question was out before she could stop herself. "I mean if you don't date, is your life a succession of one-night stands?"

That's kind of sad…

"I wouldn't say that." He frowned. *Had she pissed him off?* "Usually I know the women I sleep with. No misunderstandings that way."

The penny finally dropped. God, he must think she was so stupid. "Fuck buddies." She nodded sagely, as if that notion didn't totally squick her out, and finished off her brandy.

Jackson put his glass on the bar. "Fuck buddies implies we're friends. I don't fuck my friends."

"I'm sure they're very relieved."

For a moment he stared at her and then his lips twitched. She couldn't keep a straight face any longer, and giggled. Honestly, could their conversation get any more ridiculous if they tried?

"Do you fuck your friends, Scarlett?"

"Only if I'm dating them at the time."

He pulled a crumpled lily from her hair and tossed it onto the bar. "What do you do between dates?"

Good question. Not that she wanted to discuss it with Jackson. If she told him she didn't do casual sex, he'd want to know why she was with him tonight.

Could she really blame it all on rampant hormones? She'd gone without sex for extended periods in the past without jumping the bones of a virtual stranger, no matter how ripped he was.

Only I've never met a guy as ripped as Jackson Grayson. No way was she telling him that.

"I fight off fortune hunters."

"Fortune hunters?" He sounded disbelieving. But he hadn't grown up with the Ashford name and everything it entailed. Sometimes it seemed half the people she met only wanted to know her because of her family connections, and the other half wanted to stab her in the back for the same reason.

She gave an exaggerated sigh, so he wouldn't guess she was telling the sad truth. "It's a real pain in the ass."

He pulled her against him. "The next time a fortune hunter comes knocking, you send him to me. I guarantee he won't bother you again."

"I might just do that." She wouldn't, of course. "Maybe I should keep you on retainer."

"Maybe you should." He pulled a few more lilies from her hair and dropped them onto the carpet. Belatedly she remembered she'd wanted to freshen up. But that moment had long passed. Jackson obviously didn't see anything wrong with the way she looked so why should she worry about it?

• • •

Jackson pulled the last flower from Scarlett's hair and tossed it onto the floor. If he had any sense, he'd leave her now. They'd had their fun. And while he wasn't opposed to enjoying a lot more of what she had to offer, he'd just confirmed, as he always suspected, that Scarlett didn't go in for casual sex as a rule.

Why had she changed her mind tonight? He had no idea. And he didn't want to know.

"What's with the frown?" Scarlett walked her fingernails

up his chest. Why had he wanted to know about her sex life? Now he was obsessed by the possibility this was her first one-night stand. Instead of wanting to cut and run he was…

What the fuck was he?

Flattered.

Shit. That was a first.

"I wasn't frowning. I was thinking."

"You said you didn't have second thoughts." She undid a button on his shirt.

"I don't." Except that wasn't true. Since the minute Scarlett had walked into his office his thoughts concerning her had been a mess. He wasn't used to a woman getting inside his head like that. Luckily after tonight, when he'd gotten her out of his system, she would no longer be a problem.

In any case, he still had two more condoms in his pocket. Since Scarlett was clearly willing, they might as well take advantage of them.

"Because I wouldn't want to think I have you here under duress." She slid another button free.

"No chance of that." He pulled a glittery clip from her hair and sent it the same direction as the flowers. Her blonde curls tumbled around her shoulders in sexy disarray. "I haven't seen you naked yet."

Her fingers stilled. "Is that the only reason you're still here?" She sounded as though she wasn't sure whether to be offended or not. He traced the outline of her ear with one finger, and her long diamond earring sparkled against her neck. *Had he just slung a diamond-encrusted clip across the floor?*

"You haven't seen me naked, either."

Her frown disappeared. "That's true." There was a

husky note in her voice now. "Shall we go through to the bedroom?"

"What's wrong with the sitting room?"

She glanced at a nearby sofa. "Oh. Right. Well, let me get the lights, then."

He thought it was light enough, but if she wanted the overhead chandelier all lit up as well who was he to argue. "Allow me."

He left her standing by the bar, went to the panel and flipped the switch.

Scarlett blinked, her mouth agape. "What did you do that for?"

"What?"

"The chandelier." She waved her hand at the offending object. "I meant we needed to turn the lights *off*."

She wasn't making sense. "But then I wouldn't be able to see you."

A pained expression crossed her face. "We could keep one of the small side lamps on."

He had a better idea. "How about this?" He flipped all the switches off except for the chandelier. Rainbows scattered across the floor and walls.

"I guess that's okay." There was doubt in her voice as she watched him prowl toward her. He pulled his shirt from his pants, intending to rip it over his head. "No, stop." She gripped his wrist and a wicked smile lit up her face. "Allow *me*."

He had no problem with that. "You do know I'll return the favor."

She undid another of his buttons. "I'm counting on it."

The concentration on her face as she worked her way

down his shirt was kind of amusing. From this angle he had a view down her cleavage, and combined with the sound of her uneven breathing, the amusement was rapidly becoming outweighed by lust.

How long did it take to unbutton a shirt, for God's sake?

"There." Scarlett looked up at him. "Almost done." She undid the buttons at his cuffs and eased his shirt over his shoulders, as though he were made of glass and might shatter if she moved too quickly.

He wasn't made of glass, but he might well shatter if she didn't get a move on.

He gritted his teeth and sucked it up. She was worth the wait.

Slowly she inched his shirt over his biceps. He'd give her another minute to enjoy her power and then he'd take control—before he damn well lost it.

She drew in a sharp breath, her gaze riveted on his chest. "What happened?" Her fingers hovered over the scar, as though she was afraid to touch him.

He couldn't believe Scarlett was asking him about his old battle scars right now.

"Nothing. Just a broken bottle."

"A broken bottle?" She sounded horrified. "That's awful."

She obviously wasn't letting this go until she had all the bloody details. He should've gone with just a side lamp like she'd suggested. Maybe then she wouldn't have noticed.

"Could have been worse. Bastard was aiming for my face."

Tentatively, she touched the puckered skin with the tip of one finger. Unfortunately, he couldn't feel a thing, since his nerves there were permanently damaged.

"I hope justice was served."

"It was." But not in the way she likely thought. When Jackson had recovered from surgery, he'd paid the guy a visit. Not that he intended telling Scarlett that.

At seventeen he'd brandished his scar like a Medal of Honor, but now, nine years down the track, he knew how lucky he'd been to come out alive in that particular fight.

It had taken him another year, and a knife in the back, before he'd finally come to his senses and gotten out of the game.

"Was that the same time you broke your nose?"

What was this, twenty questions?

"No. Did that when I was fourteen." During his first official street fight, two weeks after Alex had been hauled off to juvie and their gran had moved in. On the upside, he'd won that fight and more than a fistful of dollars, but set the pattern of his life for the next four years, until the knife incident.

"Sounds like you had a dangerous youth."

"I could take care of myself." *But I wasn't able to take care of Cooper.* He shoved the guilty memory of his little brother aside, but it clawed through him all the same. "Let's just say I was dangerous to know."

"I'd say you're *still* dangerous to know."

"You'd be right."

She gave a sexy half-smile before pulling his shirt off his arms and dropping it onto the floor. Then she ran the tip of her finger along his fly.

He gripped her wrist. "Like playing games, do you?"

"I guess I do." There was a hint of laughter in her words. "What about you?"

He pressed the palm of her hand against his erection. "I always play to win, babe."

"Good to know." Her voice dripped with temptation. "Forewarned and all."

It appeared she'd forgotten he was still half dressed. With brutal economy he shoved his pants down his legs. Scarlett's gaze dropped.

"Your turn." He pulled her against him. The silk of her dress and the warmth of her body molded to his naked skin in a fuck-me-now caress. He searched for a zipper or buttons along her back, and found neither. "How the fuck does this thing come off?"

"Hooks and eyes." Her voice was uneven. "It's a nightmare."

Yeah, and it was a nightmare he had no intention of navigating. He grasped the top her dress, where it draped off her shoulders, and wrenched the silk apart.

Scarlett gasped and stiffened in his arms. "You ripped the dress." Shock spiked each word. Obviously she had never played this particular game before.

"Were you planning on wearing it again?"

"Well, *no*, but—"

He ripped the rest of the material and her dress slithered to the floor in a pool of green silk. Scarlett gaped and folded her arms across her breasts as he drank in the sight of her gorgeous body, clad in nothing but a lacy green thong and sexy stilettos.

She hitched in a ragged breath and he waited for her to slap his face or something. Not that it would make any difference. Ripping the dress off her had been fucking hot.

"That was…" She hesitated for a second. "Unexpected."

He dragged his gaze up from her heels, admiring her

legs. He knew she wasn't really that tall, but those shoes made her legs go on forever. "Unexpected is my specialty."

"Do you make a habit of tearing peoples' clothes off?"

"Only those I want to fuck."

He stifled the urge to laugh at the disbelief on her face. "Really?"

He couldn't help it. He laughed. "No, Scarlett. I've never torn a woman's dress off her before. But I can't promise I'll never do it to you again."

"If I'd known, I wouldn't have bothered to be so careful with your shirt."

The thought of her ripping his clothes off him was dangerously addictive. "You'll know next time."

There isn't going to be a next time.

Before she could remind him of that fact, he grasped her wrists and pried her arms away from her breasts.

He sucked in a breath. Her tits were gorgeous. Full and ripe, with nipples that just begged to be licked. He took a step toward her, intending to do just that, and ground out a curse.

His pants were tangled round his ankles. He toed off his shoes and tore off his socks and pants in record time, aware of how Scarlett watched. It wasn't the best performance of his life but better than tripping over his own feet. Before his brain left the building completely, he tossed a condom onto the nearby loveseat.

Scarlett let out an appreciative sigh and then dropped to a crouch. For one insane second he thought she was going to give him head, but instead she started to take off her own shoes.

"Leave them on." He grasped her arms and hauled her

upright. He never thought he had a shoe fetish before, but damn. Tonight he could understand the attraction.

"Good thinking. If I took them off I'd only reach your shoulder."

"That's not why I want you to keep them on."

"I know." Her sultry whisper coiled through his blood. "Do you want me to walk all over you?"

"Fuck no." Was she for real? "You could seriously injure me."

Her giggle was the sexiest sound he'd ever heard, and the way she slapped her hand over her mouth, in a vain effort to contain her mirth, made him harder.

"Does the thought of inflicting pain turn you on?" He glided his hands over her arms and shoulders, and then down her back to the dip of her waist. Her skin was satiny soft.

"No." A delicate shiver rippled over her wherever he touched. She speared her fingers through his hair and pressed her body against him. Her erect nipples damn near caused him to lose what little control he still had.

"You still want to find out what my mouth can do?"

"Oh, yes." It was a breathy surrender, and she tilted her head back so she could look him in the face.

He wrapped one arm around her waist to keep her still. His other hand palmed her ass. She'd felt good through her dress. Without it, he wasn't sure how long he could last.

With a throaty groan he sucked her nipple into his mouth. Her nails dug into him and she arched her back, burying his face in her scented flesh.

She is so fucking gorgeous. Slowly he sank to his knees and trailed hot kisses across her stomach.

"Your mouth is good." Her voice shook. He looked up

at her and grinned at the glazed expression on her face.

"You haven't seen anything yet."

"I'm not sure…"

"I don't go back on my word."

She hitched in a ragged breath and her pink lips parted. *Christ, that was hot.* For a second he imagined her going down on him, taking him into that sexy mouth of hers.

God yes…

But he wanted to feel her come in his mouth. Wanted her to fall apart the way she had against the tree. Wanted her clinging onto him, all wet and needy as she gasped his name. His balls tightened with unbearable need.

He dipped lower and slid her thong down her legs. A slender ribbon of pale blonde curls dusted her swollen heat and she wobbled on those insane heels of hers.

"I think I might have to sit down." Her breathy whisper was almost his undoing.

"Not yet." He stroked his thumb along her wet slit. She was so soft and silky. His heart thundered, making it hard to think straight.

Just take her now. She was ready. But he wanted her to remember this night forever. And two quickies wouldn't do it.

He palmed her ass to keep her still and swirled his tongue over her clit. She bucked and made a strangled sound of pleasure, and he tightened his hold on her.

"It's official," she panted. "You have a talented tongue."

He pulled back just enough so he could speak. "I'm going to make you scream my name."

She gave a hoarse laugh. "I don't scream."

He slid a finger into her and her moan vibrated through

her body. "You will."

"Jackson." She drew out his name in a husky whisper. *This woman is killing me.* He slid a second finger inside her and tongued her clit. She tasted so good.

He massaged her with his fingers, teasing her sweet spot. Her erratic breath, and the little sounds of pleasure she made, were all he could hear above the frantic thud of his heart.

He clutched her ass in a brutal grip, and Scarlett reared against him. She was hot and slippery and her musky scent drove him crazy. *I need to be inside her.* As her orgasm hit he pressed his tongue against her peak and her shudders vibrated through his mouth.

With a growl he stood, lifted her from the floor, and backed her onto the nearest loveseat. He hauled Scarlett onto his lap. She hung onto his shoulders, her mouth open and eyes glazed, and her hair tumbled over her damp face.

Somehow he managed to sheath himself without taking his eyes from her. "Ride me, Scarlett." It was a harsh demand. When she didn't instantly comply, he palmed her ass and lifted her from his lap.

She blinked and shifted, angling her wet slit over the head of his dick. Then she paused, and a smile of pure evil lit her flushed face.

"I didn't scream."

He laughed, and it fucking hurt. "You will by the time I'm finished with you."

Slowly she slid down his cock. "Promises." There was a faintly mocking note in her voice, but it was overshadowed by lust. Her eyes drifted shut and her lips parted as she clenched her muscles around him.

He nearly lost it right then. *So tight.* He couldn't breathe.

He held her hips, guiding her rhythm "You're fucking gorgeous." His voice was hoarse.

"So are you."

Pressure built, blinding him to everything but the way Scarlett looked and felt in his arms. *Not yet.* He fought against it, wanting this moment to last. Scarlett gasped and leaned into him, her lips brushing his. It was a barely there kiss, and it was the best fucking kiss ever.

"Jackson." Her breath scorched his mouth and all he could see were her beautiful blue eyes. "Come for me."

Raw lust ripped through him. *Can't hold on.* He pumped his release inside her and her orgasm shattered his mind.

She clung onto him, her head buried against his shoulder. He tightened his arms around her, not ready to let her go yet.

His thoughts drifted. *This feels good.* He closed his eyes and breathed in her faint scent. She was soft and warm. Her hair tickled his nose. *Funny...*

Deep inside, unease stirred. *What am I doing?* Why wasn't he trying to untangle himself from Scarlett? *Why don't I feel caged?*

Chapter Eight

Jackson wasn't sure what woke him, but as he stirred he became aware of the woman snuggled against his side. Not only that, he had his arm around her.

It took him a couple of seconds to realize his first thought hadn't been to hit the floor running.

Just like last night.

He shoved the thought aside. It didn't matter. He liked having Scarlett in his arms. He had no great urge to leave before she woke up.

And that was strange. It wasn't as though they could do anything much this morning except to part ways. After falling into bed, they'd used the last of the condoms.

His dick stirred against his thigh.

It was crazy. They'd had sex three times. He shouldn't still want her as much as he had this time yesterday. Except he did.

Her lashes fluttered. Without meaning to, he brushed a

curl from her face and then grinned down at her. Couldn't seem to help himself. She looked so cute, all sleepy eyes and bruised lips.

"Morning." Against his better judgment his arm tightened around her. "Sleep well?"

She licked her lips and gingerly stretched. Trouble was, that caused her body to rub against his. But before he could enjoy it too much, she froze, and then edged back until they were no longer plastered together.

He should be relieved she hadn't wrapped herself around him like a clinging vine—his worst nightmare when it came to waking up beside a woman. Mornings could be messy.

But an odd sense of disappointment spiked through his chest. Which didn't make any fucking sense at all.

"Morning." Her voice was smoky and did nothing to help the state of his arousal. "What's the time?"

He frowned at his watch. He couldn't believe he'd slept in so late. "Just gone eight."

"God." Scarlett tugged her fingers through her hair. He had the insane urge to fork his own fingers through her tangled curls, claim her lips once again, and sink inside her. He swallowed and resisted the temptation to grip his cock and find another method of instant relief.

Seriously. He was twenty-six years old and in control of his body's needs. With that in mind, he rescued his arm from around Scarlett, linked his hands above his head, and stretched his cramped muscles.

It didn't do a damn thing for his dick, though.

Neither did the expression on Scarlett's face as she watched him. Shit. This was getting awkward. Another reason why he avoided the morning after the night before whenever he could.

"Well, that was fun." She sat up and pulled a sheet around her in a vain attempt at modesty. He didn't know why she bothered. He'd seen plenty of her body the night before.

"Sure was." He itched to trail his fingers along the length of her naked back. Now that he thought about it, he hadn't seen her back last night. He closed his eyes for a moment but it didn't help. Her back was as sexy as her front.

"Did you want to use the shower first?" She looked over her shoulder at him. He almost told her they could use the shower together, but there was no point. If he got her under the spray, all wet and slippery, he'd want to fuck her.

"No it's okay. You go ahead. I'll clean up at home."

• • •

This is so excruciatingly embarrassing. Scarlett kept the fake smile on her face as Jackson stretched like a satisfied panther beside her. The sheet and quilt barely covered his groin and his naked torso was the stuff of wet dreams. All she wanted to do was crawl over him and lick every delicious inch of his toned body, but he'd made it crystal clear yesterday that he was only interested in one night.

The last thing she wanted was for his lingering memories of her to be of someone who didn't know when to just back the hell off.

Except she didn't have the first idea how to handle this situation. Should she suggest they have breakfast together? Grab a coffee? Or would that look as though she expected more from this encounter than they had both agreed on?

One thing was certain. He expected an answer from her. She cleared her throat and hoped her hair wasn't really as messy as it felt.

"Okay." Wow, how articulate could she get? Luckily it appeared to be enough for Jackson as he shot another bone melting smile her way before flinging back the covers and turning his back on her.

She gave a silent sigh of appreciation. His back was all bronzed and muscled and—

Her heart slammed against her ribs.

Crap, what's that? What looked like an old knife wound disfigured his lower back.

Her fingers clenched in the sheet, and she smothered the urge to touch him there. She could only imagine the kind of life he'd led if it included being attacked by both a broken bottle and a knife.

They might have had sex—and pretty mind blowing sex, at that—but the truth was, she knew almost nothing about him.

The problem was, she wanted to.

She dragged her gaze from his scar and feasted on the sight of his tight ass as he stood up and gave another R-rated stretch. Then he strolled to the bedroom door, and her hungry gaze drank in the sight of his strong thighs. She felt like the world's worst pervert, drooling over him, but couldn't help herself.

At the door he paused. She had the uncanny sense he was posing for effect, before he turned and she caught sight of his erection.

She drew up her legs and buried her burning face in the

bed sheet. Jackson Grayson was hot in bed and out of it.

She was so ready for another sweaty session with him. And that was after she'd come three—no, *four* times during the night. Usually the big O was an elusive hope shimmering on the horizon for her.

Jackson didn't just have a talented tongue. He had a talented… everything.

It was only when he touched her shoulder that she realized how long she'd been daydreaming about him. She raised her head.

Anything she might have said died in her throat at the sight of him. His black hair was disheveled, his morning stubble hypnotic, and the rakish way his shirt was undone at the throat and his tie hung in abandoned disarray beneath the collar, was just plain panty-melting.

I'm not wearing any panties.

"Do you need me to drive you home?"

She reeled in her lascivious thoughts and hoped he couldn't read her mind. "No, it's fine." Unfortunately, her voice hadn't received the memo. She sounded completely desperate. She cleared her throat and tried again. "Thanks, um, for everything."

Crap, and now he'd think she was thanking him for the sex. She hadn't meant it to sound that way.

What way had she meant it to sound?

How much champagne did I drink?

A heart-stopping smile played around his lips. "I told you I'd give full satisfaction in all areas."

He might have been referring to the services she'd hired him for. Except the gleam in his eyes told her he was referring to a lot more than that.

And she had to admit. He had certainly delivered.

"I have no complaints." She gave him a nod to underscore her remark and hoped she came across as worldly and not so totally out of her depth that she feared she was drowning. "I'd be happy to give you a reference if you ever need one."

Why won't my mouth shut up? Jackson would think she was insane.

"Thanks for the offer." He sounded on the verge of laughing. She gripped the sheet as mortification licked through her. But he didn't laugh. A frown flickered across his brow, and for one eternal moment she had an eerie certainty he was about to kiss her.

Then he straightened and backed away. Thank God for that.

Liar.

"You know where I am if you need anything," Jackson said, and then he frowned again, as though he was worried she might take him literally.

It stung. Did he really think she'd chase after him?

Even if she did want to see him again—which she didn't—there was no way she'd embarrass herself by running after a guy who so clearly wasn't interested.

"Thanks, but I'm sure I can take it from here." She smiled and nodded yet again, although she had no idea why she was nodding, except it hopefully emphasized her complete lack of intention to follow up his offer.

"Right." He took another backward step. His gaze never left hers. Silence spun between them, and the air thickened with untold promises of sex. Then he let out a measured breath. "See you around, Scarlett."

And with that, he turned and walked out of her life.

Chapter Nine

A couple of hours later, Scarlett made her way to the Presidential Suite. Her father's summons had roused her from her post-Jackson stupor enough to take a long shower. It hadn't helped to scrub either the previous night or the man himself from her mind.

Then again, did she really want to scrub him from her mind? Every time she remembered the things he'd done with his hands and tongue, delicious aftershocks rippled through her body.

She realized another satisfied smile was on her face and hastily schooled her features as her dad opened the door.

"Hey, Dad." She kissed his cheek. "All set for your honeymoon?" He was taking Clarissa to Monte Carlo because she'd never been, and it was at the top of her extensive bucket list.

"As I'll ever be." He pushed the door shut behind her and indicated she should follow him into the sitting room.

"Clarissa's having a spa treatment this morning. I wanted to speak with you alone."

Scarlett's stomach pitched. That didn't sound good. Before she could think of a suitable response he added, "I didn't see much of you at the reception last night."

She hadn't expected him to notice. She sat on a sofa opposite him and tried to come up with an acceptable excuse.

"You were otherwise occupied."

He reclined in his chair and studied her. For a man approaching sixty and who, eighteen months ago, had almost died, he looked remarkably fit. And she had to admit a lot of that credit went to Clarissa who, despite her social climbing aspirations, did make sure Scarlett's dad took care of himself.

She tucked her hair behind her ear and tried not to fidget. It was the same whenever her father turned the full force of his attention her way. Probably because he so rarely did. Usually their relationship was more of the fleeting kind, or conducted in the midst of family and relatives.

At least, it had been that way for the last ten years. She didn't remember any kind of reserve between them when her mom was alive.

Finally he spoke. "Is it serious between you and Jackson Grayson?"

For one scary second she almost said "yes", not because of the thread of regret in the back of her mind that there was nothing serious between her and Jackson at all. It was because the note of censure in her father's voice pissed her off.

Shock slithered through her. *Dad doesn't piss me off.*

She forced a smile to her lips. She'd rather die than admit

to anyone the truth of her relationship with Jackson, but she could live with a partial revelation. "Of course not. It's just a bit of fun, that's all."

Her father's watchful stance relaxed very slightly. "I'm glad to hear that, honey. Guy like that could break your heart."

"Mm." Surely her dad wasn't about to give her a lecture on her love life? He'd never even touched on the subject before. Then again, the only guys she'd dated in the past had been the sons or relatives of people in his own social sphere.

How weird he had never considered that any of *them* might break her heart.

"You know how I feel about your working at *Rose Marie*."

Scarlett frowned. What did her working at the women's shelter her mom had set up have to do with Jackson? And yes, she knew what her father thought of it.

He didn't like her getting her hands dirty. Hadn't liked her mom getting her hands dirty, either.

It wasn't a sense of duty that kept her at *Rose Marie House,* because of her mom's involvement in the shelter, or because she had volunteered alongside her mom while she was a teen. It was that she enjoyed working there. And while her original dream of becoming a lawyer—so she could help out in a more solid role by taking on pro rata cases—had fallen through due to her lack of passion for law, it was still a good feeling to know she was actually needed.

"Mom always wanted me to continue with her work."

It wasn't a lie. Guilt stabbed through her when her dad flinched.

He recovered quickly. He always did. But she'd be

kicking herself for the rest of the week for having resorted to such a dirty tactic.

"I know that. It's the reason I tolerate your insistence in spending so much time there." He might have been speaking to one of his lowly employees for all the warmth in his voice. When she was a child, had he really laughed and played with her, or was it all a fantasy her imagination had conjured over the years?

"Dad—"

"But." He cut through her interruption. "There's a difference between working alongside undesirables and inviting them into your personal life. Always remember that, Scarlett."

Injustice bubbled in her chest and her face burned. For a start, she didn't work alongside *undesirables*. They had good security at the shelter—real security, who weren't afraid to face any abusive ex who might roll up to the front door.

But it was her father's dig at Jackson that really scraped her nerves.

"Jackson Grayson isn't an undesirable." There was a touch of acid in her tone, but that wasn't what shocked her. It was the fact she'd openly disagreed with her dad.

He offered her a perfunctory smile that didn't reach his eyes. "I know his type. Out for whatever he can get. But I trust your judgment, Scarlett. You've had your fun at the expense of Edward and that's fine by me. I just wanted your assurance it was nothing serious for me to concern myself with."

Her father had noticed what had gone on between her and Edward? Maybe he wasn't as blindly besotted with Clarissa as she thought.

And as for Jackson—it wasn't serious. But her father's unjustified accusations against Jackson burned. If things were different, if she and Jackson *were* seeing each other, then the last thing she'd do would be to finish things with him just to please her dad.

• • •

It had been three days since he'd walked out on Scarlett. Jackson contemplated the ceiling of his office, his feet propped on his desk and his hands clasped behind his head. Why had he said, *you know where I am if you need anything.* It sounded like an invitation to get in touch.

Scarlett hadn't taken him up on that invitation.

Even though it hadn't been a fucking invitation.

His door opened and he was relieved to get away from his tangled thoughts, until he saw the smirk on Ella's face.

"Got a problem with one of your clients, J." She sounded so innocent that he knew she was up to something.

"What kind of problem?"

Ella sighed dramatically. "Financial."

He scowled. He knew what was coming. He also had no idea how to get out of the backlash that was sure to follow.

"Financial problem?" His brother Alex appeared at the door and squeezed his way into the room without touching Ella. "That's not like you, Jackson."

He almost asked Ella which client she was talking about. Except it was obvious who she was talking about, and he didn't want to draw any more attention to Scarlett's missing payment than absolutely necessary.

"There's no problem." He slung his brother a dark look.

"I'm on top of it."

Ella snorted. "Yeah, I'm sure you were, hon."

Alex shot Ella a probing look. "Am I missing something here?"

Ella's smile dimmed for a second. Despite Jackson's irritation at the way she had pounced on the screw up with Scarlett's check, a flash of sympathy streaked through him.

His brother was so fucking blind when it came to Ella. But if he said anything to Alex about her feelings, she would have his balls for breakfast.

"Nope." Jackson swung his legs off his desk. "I'm refunding the fee."

"Why?" Alex leaned against the wall, hands shoved into the pockets of his jeans. He might seem relaxed and the question might sound idle, but Jackson knew his brother better than that. He wouldn't let this go until he was satisfied with the answer.

"The assignment didn't go as planned."

Alex didn't move a muscle but Jackson could feel sudden tension radiate from him. Shit. This was rapidly turning into a nightmare.

"Trouble?" There was only a hint of interest in his brother's voice but it spoke volumes. The Graysons did not refund fees. And they didn't bend in the face of trouble. He should have told Ella first thing Monday morning that he was canceling the Ashford account, instead of pissing about for another two days until she discovered the discrepancy herself.

Ella might've given him hell for it, but she wouldn't have broken his confidence. Alex would never have known about the Ashford job, and this exchange wouldn't be taking place.

"Nothing I can't handle."

"I hope you're right about that." For once there was no laughter in Ella's voice. "We have policies in place for a reason."

For fuck's sake. He glared at her and she glared right back.

He hadn't intended to break policy with Scarlett.

Keep telling yourself that.

"You going tell me what's going on?"

Jackson stood. It was better than being psychologically disadvantaged by having to look up at Alex while his integrity was shredded.

"Things got heated. So I'm canceling the account. Satisfied?"

The resulting silence hurt his eardrums. Finally Alex spoke. "Tell me you didn't screw a client."

"I'm not discussing my sex life with you."

"Christ." Alex pushed himself away from the wall. "You better fucking sort this out, Jackson." His eyes narrowed, as though something else had occurred to him. "There's nothing serious going on between you, is there?"

"It was a one-time thing." Okay so technically it had been three times. He wasn't going into details. "Ella, can you return the deposit into the client's account?"

"Sure." There was a chill in her voice.

His brother and friend were right. Didn't mean he had to like it. In fact, he had the powerful urge to go punch something hard and unyielding.

An hour later, when Ella left to go to some animal rights rally, and Alex disappeared to the club he'd bought last year, Jackson unlocked the drawer in his desk and took out Scarlett's check. All he needed to do was rip it in half and send it back to her in the mail with a carefully worded note.

It was the note that was giving him a headache. Maybe he could just send the check back with a compliments slip.

Yeah, classy.

In the end he did what he'd been fighting against doing from the moment he'd left Scarlett in the hotel.

He picked up his cell and called her.

Chapter Ten

Scarlett stifled a yawn and feigned interest as her cousin Livia gushed over the steamy hook up she'd enjoyed over the weekend. It appeared Scarlett wasn't the only one who'd gotten laid at her father's wedding.

Only difference being, she had no intention of telling anyone about it. Unlike Livia's conquest, Jackson had expressed no interest in seeing her again.

She'd known that from the outset. *So for God's sake get over it.*

Their waiter unobtrusively replenished their drinks. The Italian restaurant was exclusive, and she and her girlfriends came there for lunch once a month. The primary reason why the Ashford cousins, and equally privileged select friends, got together was to network for their pet charities. While some last minute details about the upcoming annual ball to raise funds for *Rose Marie House* had been finalized, today had been mainly about sharing wedding gossip.

This group of friends was one of the few where they could say anything, confident nothing would get leaked to press not controlled by Ashford Communication.

"And what about that gorgeous man you pulled out at the last moment?" asked her cousin, Jade, who was almost thirty and recently divorced. "Edward was so pissed. It was hysterical."

"Nice one in the eye for Clarissa," Livia said. "Manipulative bitch."

"Yes, but where did you *find* him?" Harley was the granddaughter of a movie mogul and the same age as Scarlett, and she looked a little offended. They were, after all, good friends and had grown up together. They'd even gone to the same boarding school.

"Through mutual acquaintances." At least that was the truth. "It's just really casual. Nothing serious."

"It didn't look that way on the dance floor." Jade leaned across the table. "You looked fucking combustible together."

"Don't tell me you're friends with benefits?" Harley sounded flabbergasted. "Since when have you ever done that? My God, Scarlett. Did you *sleep* with him?"

Somehow, when she'd come up with the idea of hiring a man to keep Edward and Clarissa off her back, she hadn't considered the fallout among her friends. Of course they'd want every dirty detail. Especially when Jackson Grayson wasn't anyone they could hunt down through the intertwined branches of a few well-connected family trees.

"By the look on her face I don't think much *sleeping* went on," Livia said. "So how long have you been hooking up?"

Scarlett took a fortifying sip of wine. To lie or not to lie, that was the question. If she could just get over the fact she'd hired Jackson in the first place, would she find it so hard to tell her friends about the hottest night she'd ever had?

Luckily her cell chose that moment to ring, and with a silent sigh of relief she pulled it from her purse.

Jackson Grayson.

It was slightly freaky the way he'd contacted her at the very moment she'd been talking about him. Gingerly she answered. "Hi."

"Hey, Scarlett. It's Jackson Grayson."

Even if his name hadn't come up with his number, she'd know that sinfully sexy voice anywhere. She licked her lips and then caught sight of eight pairs of eyes avidly watching her.

It was obvious they'd all guessed exactly who she was talking to.

"Yes, hi." She cleared her throat. "Everything okay?"

She couldn't imagine why he'd called. But no way was she going to ask him when she had an audience hanging on every word. She'd just have to somehow bluff her way through.

"That's why I got in touch. There's a hitch with the financials."

She literally felt the blood rush to her head, heating her cheeks until she knew she must look like an overripe tomato. She transferred her cell to her other hand and angled away from the table. If anyone had overheard that comment she would *die*.

"Uh-huh." Her voice sounded strangled. Maybe she should just finish this conversation outside. Except she wasn't sure her legs would support her. "And why is that?"

Maybe he'd lost the check. It was the only reason she could think of why there would be a problem. The deposit had gone through but he'd told her he wouldn't cash the balance until after the job was done.

The job had well and truly been done.

"I don't want to discuss it over the phone. Can you come to the office?"

His words swam through her mind, not making much sense. "What, now?"

"Yeah, if that's not a problem."

It was no problem at all ditching her friends to go and see him. The question was, why should she?

He's hot.

"Scarlett?" He said her name in a way that conjured up naked bodies, tangled sheets, and mind-blowing orgasms. Who was she trying to kid? She could keep it platonic. She wasn't a sex crazed nympho who was going to jump his bones the second he opened the door to her.

"Sure. No problem."

"Great." Was that a note of relief in his voice or was it just her rampant imagination? "How long will you be?"

She calculated the distance in her head. It was just gone two, so the traffic wouldn't be too bad. "About twenty minutes."

· · ·

Jackson prowled the reception area and reminded himself for the third time that the only reason he'd called Scarlett to the office was so he could return the check to her in person. It had nothing to do with the fact that he kept thinking about her, at all kinds of odd moments during the day.

It was one night. It was over. This would be the last time he'd need to see her.

Which was why he'd called her in the middle of the day, to avoid temptation. Just because he'd waited until he was alone in the office was beside the point. He had no intention of allowing his brothers to ever see Scarlett, although he wasn't exactly certain why. Normally, he wouldn't care.

Then again, he'd never slept with a client before. Refunding her fee wouldn't wipe out that fact, but at least he wouldn't feel like she'd paid him for more than being a bodyguard.

"Fuck." He raked his hand through his hair but it didn't ease the throb in his head.

Once this was done there would be no further need to contact Scarlett Ashford again. His sense of having been bought would vanish and his ego could recover.

He was still smirking over the state of his fragile ego when the door buzzed.

Keep it professional. Sure, he could do that. He opened the door…and his principles went to hell.

Scarlett wore a short, plum colored dress with matching heels. They weren't as spiky as the ones she'd worn for the wedding but they still managed to give him dirty thoughts. Her hair was sleek and the elusive hint of her perfume had the power to knock his common sense flying. She looked elegant and untouchable.

He had the urge to slide his hand up her skirt…

Stop. This is business.

"Jackson." She smiled at him but there was a definite reserve in her tone. He reeled in the suicidal desire to pull her into his office and bend her over his desk.

"Come in." He stepped back and resisted the temptation to kiss her in greeting. He didn't want her getting the wrong idea, and if he touched her, he wasn't sure he'd be able to let her go.

She took a deep breath and glanced around the empty reception area. "So you said there was a problem?"

He shut the door and mentally slammed his forehead against the reinforced metal. Had he really forgotten just how irresistible Scarlett was?

"Not really a problem." He swung around and jammed his hands in his pockets to keep them away from her. "Come on into the office."

She clutched her purse against her thigh and walked ahead of him. Every step she took caused her dress to caress the curve of her ass. Her legs were bare and all he could think about was the way she'd wrapped them around him the last time they'd had sex.

He pulled his hands from his pockets. It was too damn uncomfortable to walk straight otherwise. He could only hope she hadn't noticed his erection. It hardly gave the right impression.

"No Ella today?" Scarlett turned to face him as he followed her into the office and kicked the door shut behind him.

"She has the afternoon off." Shit, did that sound as though he'd planned this encounter with Scarlett? If so, she didn't seem pissed by the possibility of being alone with him. "You didn't have any problem taking time off work to come here?"

He had no idea what she did, or whether she even

worked at all.

Scarlett sat on the chair and crossed her legs. "I was only having lunch with the girls. Just a monthly thing we do."

He should have guessed. Women like Scarlett Ashford didn't do anything as common as have a regular job. They did lunch and raised funds for charities.

Not that he had anything against those who supported charities. God knows they were needed. But he and his brothers had once relied on charity handouts to survive, and the whole thing just kind of burned.

He parked his ass on the edge of his desk and stretched out his legs. There was barely an inch between his foot and Scarlett's peek-a-boo shoe that showed off her plum-colored toenails.

"No more trouble from Edward?" Why was he making conversation with her? He should just give her the check and see her off the premises.

Soon.

Scarlett smiled and her gaze caught his. "Haven't heard a peep from him since the wedding. Guess my plan worked."

"Glad to have been of assistance."

The tip of her tongue peeked between her lips. She appeared to be considering her reply. He tried not to focus on her mouth because that brought up all sorts of memories he was trying so hard to forget. Easier said than done.

"Although…" Scarlett paused, and he finally managed to look her in the eye again. "There is one area in which I feel you didn't quite deliver."

Shock punched through him. Of all the things he might have imagined Scarlett to say, that had definitely not been on his short list.

"I didn't deliver?" What the fuck was she talking about? As if to mock the way he was trying to obliterate the memories from the weekend, he recalled her breathy gasps and the way her body had quivered when she came.

His dick stirred. Hell. That's what this was. Pure hell. He should've stuffed the check in the mail and left it at that.

"You promised I would scream. And I didn't."

Chapter Eleven

I did not just say that.

The comical disbelief on Jackson's face confirmed that she had.

Scarlett resisted the urge to cover her face with her hands. What was it about Jackson that caused her to lose her normal inhibitions? When it came to him, her common sense went AWOL.

From the second he opened the door, all her good intentions to keep everything safely platonic had gone up in smoke. He might not have touched her, but the heat in his eyes and the tension radiating from him said it all.

It was too late to back down now. She had to brazen it out, or risk looking like a complete loser.

"No, you didn't." He leaned forward and grasped the arms of her chair. "I need to fix that."

Her heart thudded against her ribs. He wasn't laughing at her.

All she had to do was remain calm and act as though she was used to making such statements. Except her mind had gone blank and all she could think of was ripping Jackson's shirt off and licking his hard, toned body from the tip of his crooked nose to the ends of his toes.

Words were overrated. She reached out and circled the nearest shirt button. Even through the cotton the heat of his body warmed her and it caused all sorts of havoc between her thighs.

He didn't move toward her but his biceps tensed and his breathing became uneven. It was all the encouragement she needed to tug his button free.

"Thought you were going to rip my shirt off me the next time." His voice was smoky and sent curls of need spiraling through her blood.

"Do you want me to?"

His gaze seared her from the inside out. "Seems we're all about keeping our promises here, Scarlett."

Until she met Jackson, sex had been neat and tidy. She wasn't sure she ever wanted to go back to that kind of sex.

She trailed the tip of her finger from the base of his throat to where she'd opened his shirt. A sprinkling of hair dusted his pecs and tickled her finger.

"I always keep my promises."

His predatory smile sent a shiver of anticipation over her bare skin. He leaned in closer, his jaw scraping along hers, and whispered in her ear, "Prove it."

That wasn't a command. That was a dare.

She gripped his shirt. He teased her earlobe with the tip of his tongue. It was mindlessly distracting. She took a deep breath and yanked the material apart.

There was a satisfying ripping sound as buttons scattered. Their gazes clashed, and the air in her lungs evaporated.

"My turn."

. . .

Scarlett shuddered and her grip on his shirt tightened. Did she think he'd rip this dress as he had the last one? There was a time and place for that sort of thing, and this wasn't it.

He slid the spaghetti straps over her shoulders and along her arms before hooking a finger into the front of her dress and tugging it down. A strapless plum-colored bra cupped her breasts, the lace barely covering her nipples.

He hadn't asked her here today for this, but no way was he going to pass up the kind of challenge she'd issued.

He sank to his knees and she wrapped her legs around his thighs, tugging him closer. He wanted her naked, but this was so fucking sexy.

"Should you lock the door?" She forked her fingers through his hair, pulling his head back.

"No one's coming back today." Alex would be hours at his club and Cooper was away for the week on a job. "You can scream as loud as you want, babe."

She slid her hands underneath his shirt to grasp his shoulders. "Maybe I'll make you scream instead."

"Nothing could make me scream." He traced the edge of her bra where it cradled her flesh. "You can try and make me roar, though."

"I hope these walls are soundproofed."

He cradled her hips and sucked her nipple into his mouth. Even through the material of her bra she tasted as good as he remembered. He moved upward, trailing kisses across her breasts and collarbone until he reached her throat. She sighed and tilted her head. The primitive urge to suck that tender skin and brand her neck thundered through him.

So fucking tempting.

He gently nipped her throat, not enough to leave a mark, and she gasped and arched toward him. Her nails dug in his shoulders, and when she opened her eyes, he smiled.

"The walls aren't soundproofed."

She dragged her nails down his chest. Damned if she wasn't marking *him*. "I don't care."

Neither did he. With one swift movement he stood, bringing her with him. Her dress fell to her hips, the spaghetti straps draped over her wrists.

He moved in for the kiss. And heard the outer door to the office slam shut.

Scarlett jerked back as though she'd been electrocuted. Disbelief pounded through him in furious tandem with the lust that scorched his reason.

What the hell was Alex doing back? It wouldn't be Ella. Once she pledged her time to one of her animal causes it'd take the apocalypse to make her change her plans.

"Shit." He shoved his shirt back into his pants but there was nothing he could do about the state of his missing buttons. Scarlett was hastily straightening her dress. But instead of looking pissed or, worse, upset, she appeared as though she fought back the urge to giggle.

Despite his frustration, he gave a reluctant grin. It could have been worse. He could've had Scarlett over his desk when Alex walked in.

"Stay here." His voice was low and he couldn't resist a

fleeting kiss on her lips as he went to the door. "I'll get rid of him."

Scarlett pressed her lips together. Yeah, she was definitely trying not to laugh. He winked at her, before opening the door and entering the reception area, where Alex was going through Ella's desk.

Jackson pulled his door closed and then folded his arms. At least that hid most of the damage to his shirt.

Alex ignored him and crouched down to look under Ella's desk. What the fuck was he doing?

"You lost something?"

Alex stood and slung Jackson a scowl. "Ella forgot her purse."

Jackson frowned. He'd obviously missed something. "She did what?"

"She got to the rally and realized she'd left her purse here. She called me and asked me to pick it up for her."

"Right." Ella had remembered to take her cell and car keys, but somehow hadn't taken her purse with her. He watched his brother finally pull open the bottom drawer of her desk, from which he then extracted Ella's monster-sized purse. "And you're going to the rally to give it to her?"

Alex placed Ella's purse on her desk and eyed it as though it might bite. "Yeah. You know what she's like. Half her life is in her purse. She's lost without it."

It wasn't worth responding to that. Couldn't Alex see she had planned this? His older brother was no fool when it came to women. Except when it came to Ella.

Jackson would never be so clueless if a woman gave him that many signs. No—he'd be out the door in a nanosecond.

He heard his door open and swung round to see Scarlett

stroll into reception. No one would guess just minutes ago she'd been half undressed and clawing his chest.

"I won't take up any more of your time, Jackson." She smiled at him and held out her hand. "Thank you for seeing me." He glanced at her hand before gingerly unfolding his right arm. Her thumb stroked his as they touched, before she pulled back.

Alex had an unreadable expression on his face. Jackson silently groaned.

Still keeping his left arm plastered across his chest in the vain hope Alex wouldn't notice the state of his shirt, he stepped between them.

"Ms. Ashford, this is my brother, Alex." He glared at his brother, daring him to say anything incriminating.

He caught the amused glance Scarlett shot him at his formal introduction, before she held out her hand to Alex. "Mr. Grayson," she said. "I'm pleased to meet you."

Alex took her hand. "The pleasure is all mine."

Scarlett turned to him and offered another spellbinding smile. "Goodbye," she said, and before it fully hit him that she really was leaving, she walked out the door.

"Tell me she's not one of *the* Ashfords." There was a dangerous note in Alex's voice. Jackson spared his brother a glance before returning his attention to the exit. Had she really left? Or was she going to wait outside for him? He'd told her to stay in the office. Why had she come out in any case?

"Jackson."

He turned back to Alex. If Scarlett thought he was going to chase after her, she was wrong. What the fuck had his brother just asked him?

"Yes, she's one of those Ashfords."

"Let me get this straight." Alex didn't raise his voice. He never raised his voice, but Jackson knew he was fucking mad. Tough shit. He wasn't feeling especially great himself right now. "You didn't just hit on a client. You hit on a client who happens to belong to the Ashford media empire."

Irritation spiked through him. "They won't publish anything that hints at a scandal involving one of their own, if that's what you're getting at."

"What I'm getting at, *Jackson*" — Alex emphasized his name, a sure sign he was losing his cool — "is you opened us up to allegations of sex for hire with the sleaziest media corporation in the world."

"For fuck's sake." Jackson forgot about holding his shirt together and Alex's condemning glance slid along his chest, which didn't improve Jackson's mood at all.

"So you've returned her check?"

He hadn't returned her fucking check. Fuck it. "That's why she was here. So we could conclude our business."

"Looks like it." Once again, Alex skimmed a glance along his gaping shirt. "She's hot. I get it. But a woman like her isn't worth the long-term hassle."

"Long-term hassle?" Jackson didn't know why his brother's remarks were riling him up so badly, but they were. "What the hell are you talking about? I don't fucking do long-term."

But it wasn't that comment that was pissing him off. It was the dismissive way Alex had said *a woman like her.*

Alex didn't even know Scarlett. She might be a member of the Ashford clan, but she didn't act like an entitled bitch. If he didn't know her background he would never have guessed she belonged to one of the most powerful families in the western world.

"Fine." Alex lifted Ella's purse from her desk and shoved it under his arm. "I'm just pointing out the obvious, since it appears to have bypassed you."

Jackson gritted his teeth and reined in his temper. If there was one thing the brothers never did, it was interfere in each other's sex life. Logically he knew Alex was only concerned in case things backfired onto the firm, but screw logic.

He had unfinished business when it came to Scarlett, and he wasn't just thinking about the check he needed to return.

It wasn't as though there was anything serious between them. By her reaction today she found the whole thing an enjoyable game. When she got tired of slumming, she'd move on.

Suited him. He gave them a couple of weeks, tops, until the novelty wore off.

After Alex left the office, a sense of unease gnawed through Jackson.

Scarlett never gave the impression she was slumming it. It was crazy, but he felt kind of guilty for even thinking that about her. She might live a privileged existence with what he considered shallow concerns but he could hardly hold that against her.

He took a deep breath and exhaled slowly. Why was he trying to analyze what was going on between him and Scarlett? It was sex, pure and simple. The only reason he was getting caught up in all this psychobabble crap was because Alex had rubbed him up the wrong way.

He wanted to see her again. There was no reason to put

the moment off. He pulled out his cell and punched up her number.

. . .

Scarlett took a reviving sip of her iced coffee and then sank back against the padded seat in the coffee shop. Adrenaline still raced through her, and on second thought, adding caffeine to her system probably wasn't such a great idea.

Before she could stop herself, an incredulous grin curved her lips. She couldn't believe Jackson's brother had almost caught them in the act. She should be dying of embarrassment, but all she could think about was how much she wanted to see Jackson again.

Not that she was going to contact him. She'd given him the perfect excuse to get in touch if he wanted to.

He wouldn't let her challenge go uncontested.

Her cheeks heated and she took another sip of her drink to cool herself down. Was she really going to rely on that to keep Jackson interested? If it weren't so funny it would be tragic.

By spinning this out, she was asking for trouble.

She had the feeling the more she saw him, the more she'd want him.

She'd cross that bridge when she came to it. In any case, there was still the possibility he wouldn't call her. Despite the way things had been left between them.

As if in answer to that particular question, her cell rang.

It was Jackson.

Chapter Twelve

Scarlett rolled her shoulders and stretched her arms over her head. Dealing with the mountains of admin work at the shelter was a full-time task, but at least it was Friday afternoon. She had a couple of hours before she was due at her cousin Livia's, but she wished she was seeing Jackson instead.

Tomorrow would mark their three-week anniversary. Not that she'd mentioned that to him. It hinted at commitment, and she was starting to think he had a paranoid aversion to the idea of anything that wasn't transparently transient.

Not that he'd ever said as much to her. It was more the way he never suggested they actually go out anywhere. They met, they had sex, they talked about unimportant crap, and then they went their separate ways.

There was no denying the clandestine nature of the affair was exciting. They took it in turns to choose which motel they'd meet at. Until she started seeing Jackson she'd never ever given a motel a second glance. And the sex was as phenomenal as their very first night together. But he had never invited her to his home, so she hadn't invited him to hers.

She sighed and tried to refocus on her work. There was no future with Jackson. She'd gone into this with her eyes well and truly open. The only problem was, she'd been right.

I'm having fun and I'd like more.

It went deeper than just wanting him for his ripped body and talented tongue. Sometimes she had the terrible urge to confide in him—just silly things really. Nothing earth shattering. But she never did, because she wasn't sure she could hide her hurt if his response was one of careless indifference.

The sound of male voices in the hall distracted her. The shelter was a large old house her mom had renovated almost thirty years ago, and the small room they used as an office was at the front of the property.

Is that Jackson?

Great, now she was hearing his voice. *Stop thinking about him.*

As if her thoughts materialized, there he was, walking past her door.

It really was Jackson.

For a second she sat there, stunned. He'd been there once before, nearly a month ago, when he'd rescued his friend Tessa and refused to leave until she was given refuge.

Scarlett hadn't been there, of course, but the fact Jackson and the shelter's manager knew each other from way back—plus his promise to help out for no charge if they ever needed additional security—had swayed the manager into fast-tracking the paperwork. When Scarlett had gone into work the next day, she'd heard all about it from a couple of the other volunteers. That was when she first had the idea to hire a hot bodyguard as her fake date.

She sat there for another minute or so and then couldn't help herself. She went out into the hall and followed the sound of his voice to the living room. He was sprawled on the floor, and Tessa's two little kids were swarming over him.

He looked completely at ease, as though he was used to the company of small children. She would never have guessed it. A small pain drove through the center of her chest as she leaned against the doorframe while Jackson talked to Tessa.

It was hardly a revelation, but the truth was, she knew so little about him. That wasn't why the strange sense of loss cut through her, though.

Jackson clearly didn't want her to know anything personal about him. He hadn't even told her any more about the dojo he owned, although she'd done her own research on it and had even signed the petition protesting the redevelopment.

She was getting in too deep. If she had any sense, she'd finish things with him now, before he had the chance to break her heart.

At that precise moment, Jackson rolled over, still clutching one of the children, and his gaze clashed with hers. And in that second, she knew there was no way she was going to do the sensible thing when it came to Jackson Grayson.

. . .

It wasn't often anything could literally leave Jackson speechless, but seeing Scarlett in the doorway came damn close. He remained motionless for a moment, as he took in her faded skinny jeans and sleeveless tee, and the way she'd pulled her hair back into a ponytail.

He'd never seen her so casual before. Whenever they met up she looked like she'd stepped off a catwalk. And he liked it. It was part of what made Scarlett Ashford so irresistible.

That classy, perfect image combined with her down to earth personality was a real turn-on.

And now she'd turned all that on its head. Even without makeup she still managed to look unbelievably hot.

"Hi." There was an odd expression on her face, as though she'd been watching him for quite a while before he'd become aware of her.

"Hi, yourself." He sat up, wrapping his arms around the kids as they tried to strangle him. "Didn't expect to see you here." Was there some charity function going on that he'd missed? She didn't look as though she was attending a charity function. He couldn't figure it out at all.

"How come you know Suz?" Tessa said as she pulled the kids off him.

Suz? He eyed Scarlett, not sure how he felt about the fact she used a fake name. But why had she? Which brought him back to his original question.

What the fuck is she doing here?

"Jackson and I met a few weeks ago." Scarlett tucked her hands into her jeans pockets. She sounded as though they were mere acquaintances. He wasn't sure why that rubbed him up the wrong way, but for some reason it did.

It wasn't as though he wanted her to announce to one of his oldest friends they were lovers.

But just lately it had been kind of... bugging him that they never did anything more than have sex, which was stupid because that was the way he wanted things.

He stood, and shoved his own hands into his pockets. "We're just friends," he confirmed.

Did that make Scarlett his fuck buddy?

The possibility that was how she saw them annoyed the crap out of him. Christ. What was the matter with him? Was he coming down with something?

The skeptical look on Tessa's face didn't help either.

Scarlett straightened. "Well, I didn't mean to interrupt. Catch you later." She turned and disappeared along the hall. He was sorely tempted to follow her.

"Just friends?" There was a disbelieving note in Tessa's voice. "You don't get that look on your face when you're talking to *just friends*, J."

He and Tessa had known each other for more than fifteen years. They'd been great friends until she'd hooked up with some fucking loser who lost his shit if Tessa so much as glanced at another guy. The same loser who'd ended up shoving a knife in Jackson's back.

It had taken Tessa too many years and a whole lot of courage to finally leave that jerk, and Jackson would move hell and earth to make sure she was safe. But he couldn't find the words to tell her about Scarlett.

He changed the subject but couldn't get Scarlett out of his mind. Finally he caved and left Tessa, pulling out his cell as he made his way to the front door. He and Scarlett were next seeing each other on Monday night, but he needed to talk to her before then.

As he passed the small front office, he stopped dead.

Scarlett sat at the desk, her chin propped in her hand, gazing out of the window.

Did she *work* here? He couldn't get his brain around it. Why would a socialite like Scarlett Ashford work in a women's shelter?

When she turned toward him there was a pensive expression on her face. Then she smiled, and he wondered if he'd imagined it.

He went into the office and closed the door behind him. There were a dozen questions buzzing through his mind, but he knew exactly where to start.

"Suz?"

She leaned back in her chair. "My full name is Scarlett Suzanna. Mom always called me Suz. That's how everyone here always knew me so it just stuck over the years."

Over the *years*? How long had she been doing this? And why hadn't he known about her middle name? The internet search he'd done on her before taking on the case had been cursory at best, and since they'd been seeing each other he hadn't done any more digging. It didn't feel right.

You didn't even know her full name.

He couldn't figure out why it was such a big deal.

"You came here with your mom?" Her mom was dead, but that was all he knew. That did come up on the initial search about her.

"Yes."

He waited, but it appeared that was all she had to say on the matter. Irritation licked through him. Why didn't she want to tell him anything about her personal life?

You know why.

They never shared the personal stuff. They'd laid down

the ground rules right from the start, and despite it being three weeks tomorrow since they'd first spent the night together, in reality this was all just an extended one-night stand.

"Well." There was an oddly hesitant note in Scarlett's voice and she was giving him the weirdest look. As though she wasn't sure he wanted to hear whatever it was she was about to say.

When had he ever not been interested in anything she'd said to him?

"Yeah?"

She took a deep breath. "My mom helped establish *Rose Marie House* after her dad died and my grandmother was finally free of him."

Was she telling him her grandmother had been a victim of domestic abuse?

He knew abuse crossed all social and economic boundaries, but he'd only personally encountered it in his own neighborhood. It was hard to imagine that kind of ugliness had touched Scarlett's family.

"Right." As a response it was grossly inadequate, but he was still struggling to process the fact that Scarlett obviously had a whole lot more going on in her life than he'd arrogantly assumed.

She dropped her gaze, and closed her laptop. A blush stained her cheeks. He didn't know why she was so uncomfortable. Was it because she just realized she'd given him an unintentional glimpse into her private life?

That stung.

"So you help out here sometimes?" It was stating the obvious but he didn't know how else to get her to open up about what she did.

"Three days a week." She looked up at him. "This is how I first heard about *Graysons'* — when you brought Tessa in. You see how I couldn't explain that to you at the time?"

"Confidentiality."

"Yes. And once a week I'm in the *Rose Marie* Boutique. One of the best thrift shops in LA. I have plenty of contacts and I know how to use them."

"I bet. Why didn't you tell me about this before?"

"You never asked."

No, he hadn't. The fact she cared enough to roll up her sleeves and pitch in, when all he thought she did with her days was get manicures and highlights, made him feel…

I don't know. He didn't have the words. All he knew was that, prejudiced by her background, he'd misjudged her. How could he tell her he admired the work she did, when he couldn't even figure out what he meant in his head?

"You're an amazing woman, Scarlett." *Yeah, she is.* The most amazing woman he'd ever met. But it didn't cover what he really *meant*.

"Oh." She smiled as though she wasn't too sure about his comment. "Thanks. I'm not *that* amazing, you know."

"Yes, you are. You don't have to do this. But you still do."

"Well,…" She gave an embarrassed shrug and stared at the desk. "I like being useful."

He slid his finger beneath her chin and gently raised her face until he could gaze into those beautiful blue eyes of hers. "They're lucky to have you."

And so am I.

It was three days until they were supposed to get to-gether again. He didn't want to wait that long. In fact, he'd wanted them to hook up tonight, but Scarlett had told him she was busy all weekend. He watched her as she tidied up her desk and chewed over the thought hovering in his mind.

They never went out together in public. It was always about the sex.

Not that he was complaining. But right then he had the strangest urge to show her off to the world.

This woman is mine.

"You got time to go for a coffee?"

Chapter Thirteen

Scarlett dropped the work diary onto the floor. He bent down and picked it up and she simply watched him with disbelief on her face.

He resisted the urge to back up to the door and hit the road. He put the diary on her desk, and then shoved his hands into his pockets.

It didn't matter if she said no.

"Uh, sure." She pushed a stray curl behind her ear. It was clear she was uncomfortable with the idea of going out somewhere with him. Yet she hadn't minded people seeing them together at the wedding. "You mean now?"

He thought that was obvious. "If you're done here."

"Yes, I'm done." Unless he was mistaken she looked as though she was trying not to laugh. "Although this sounds dangerously like a date to me, Jackson."

The thought didn't paralyze him.

"Just a coffee between friends."

"I thought you didn't have sex with your friends."

He didn't. Mixing sex into the dynamic was the best way to ruin a good friendship. But where did that leave Scarlett? This—whatever it was—had lasted three weeks. He enjoyed her company even when they weren't sharing mind-blowing orgasms.

It was a revelation. But he could live with it.

"Guess this one time I'll make an exception."

At the coffee shop, they found a table by the window and ordered. Scarlett sat opposite him and he hooked his foot around hers. She ran her other foot along his calf.

I want to take her back to my place. What was she doing this weekend anyway?

"Oh." Scarlett straightened and stopped playing foot-sies. "I keep forgetting to tell you. My deposit was refunded into my account weeks ago. Was that the accounting error you were talking about the other week?"

He still hadn't returned her check to her. It didn't make sense. It was almost as though the check was a guarantee of seeing Scarlett again.

I don't need an excuse to see her.

"No. I asked Ella to refund the deposit. Seeing how the night ended, it made me feel cheap."

"Trust me, you did not come cheap."

He leaned into her space. "I wouldn't want you to get the wrong idea about me."

She met him across the table. Any closer and their lips would touch. "And what idea is that?"

"That you could buy me for a few dollars."

Her lips twitched. "That's good to know."

Their coffee arrived and he watched Scarlett take a sip. She closed her eyes and savored the flavor before licking her lips and giving a sigh of satisfaction.

How could she make something so ordinary look so sexy?

"How're things going in the fight to save your dojo?"

They'd never discussed personal stuff like that before. He didn't think she'd be interested.

"Not too bad." Did she know who one of the leading voices in the call for the redevelopment was? "Looks like your Edward Saunders is banking on this going ahead to make his career."

"I think we've established he's not *my* Edward." Scarlett's response confirmed that she had known of Saunders's involvement. He wasn't sure whether that meant anything or not. "And I'd say he's going to be disappointed in the career department then, wouldn't you?"

"If I've got anything to do with it."

"Although…" Scarlett hesitated and bit her lip. "He does have his fingers in a great many bureaucratic pies."

He already knew that. The guy was a smarmy little shit who had been ruthlessly using the new contacts his cousin Clarissa's marriage to an Ashford had opened up.

"I'm not worried about his sticky fingers." It wasn't exactly true, but he found it oddly endearing that Scarlett was concerned on his behalf. "I have contacts of my own, and I'm not afraid to use them."

She blinked at him and then gave another one of her sexy smiles. "I bet," she said, and then laughed.

A crazy idea hit him. "Do you want to go visit my dojo?"

. . .

They went in Jackson's car. Scarlett tried to keep the grin off her face, but couldn't help herself.

In the space of half an hour she and Jackson had shared more personal details than they had over the last three weeks. She'd taken a chance by telling him about why her mom had established the shelter, knowing she could be setting herself up for a fall. But instead he'd been interested.

And now he was taking her to see his dojo. She didn't know why she was so excited by the thought, except for the fact it had to mean he was becoming more invested in their relationship-that-wasn't-a-relationship.

Jackson parked in a small lot behind the shops. As they strolled toward the street he threaded his fingers through hers and pressed the back of her hand against his thigh. Even after all the wild nights of sex they'd shared, the simple touch of his hand still sent electric tingles over her bare arm.

He unlocked the door and she went inside. "So what martial arts do you teach?" She turned to him, as a thought suddenly occurred to her. "Do *you* actually teach?" He might do that, for all she knew.

"No. I hire locally. Aikido, Judo, and self-defense."

He showed her the small changing areas at the back of the hall. "Are all your classes full?" she asked.

"They all have waiting lists." There was a touch of frustration in his voice. "I'd like to accept everyone, but there's a limited amount of room here."

"This must turn over a nice profit." She didn't know

what the rent was on the place but compared to most other parts of the city it had to be reasonable.

He gave her a crooked smile as he pushed open the door to what turned out to be a tiny office. "I'm not in this for the profit. It's subsidized up to its ass in grants. Most of the students can't afford to pay the fees to attend. So they don't."

Framed certificates, many with his name on them, lined one wall. Jackson might not teach any classes, but going by the recognition he'd received in Aikido, he looked more than qualified.

"So really this is a charity." If that angle was handled right, it would really screw up Edward's plans.

"We don't call it a charity." There was an edge in Jackson's voice.

"I'm sorry. I didn't mean any offense. I'm just thinking—"

"I know you didn't." He took her hand again and tugged her toward him. "I had this dream of opening a place like this for years. Somewhere the local kids can go and learn how to defend themselves in a safe environment. Get them off the streets for a few hours."

For a moment Jackson looked strangely vulnerable and she resisted the urge to wrap her arms around him and hug him tight. If she did, this moment might shatter.

"I finally got this place up and running last year. And for the last six months we've been battling this redevelopment shit."

"Well." Scarlett squeezed his fingers. "You can add me to Team Jackson if you like. I'm not bad at raising awareness for good causes."

He backed her up against his desk. "Will you call on all the old girls from your alma mater to help out?"

He was gently mocking her, but it was his defense mechanism. He'd shown her a side to himself he hadn't intended to.

"You know, I went to a regular school until I was fourteen." Until her mom died and her dad could hardly bear to look at her. "I was only at boarding school for the final four years." At least her father had sent her to the same one her friend Harley attended. She wasn't sure she would've survived otherwise.

"A regular school, huh?" He trailed a finger along the line of her jaw.

"At least it was a day school." "Regular" was probably pushing it, since she'd gone to an exclusive girls' school since kindergarten.

His body shook with a silent laugh. "I guess regular is subjective."

"Isn't everything?" She wound her arms around his neck. "Who else has keys to this place?"

"Why?"

She sank against his hard body, rose up onto her toes, and whispered in his ear. "I have this fantasy of taking you across your desk."

Chapter Fourteen

Jackson tugged her tight against his body. By the way his erection dug into her stomach, her comment had hit all the right buttons.

"That's my line." His voice was dark and dangerous and she shivered with anticipation. "I've wanted you over my desk since the first moment you walked into *Graysons*."

"I'll tell you a secret." She speared her fingers through his hair, loving the way the silky strands caressed her skin. "That's how long I've had my fantasy."

"Scarlett, babe." There was an irresistible hint of laughter in his tone. "That's no secret, trust me."

She gasped in mock indignation and pulled back. He was grinning at her in that wickedly sexy way that always managed to turn her knees weak.

"I managed to hide how I felt very well, I think." At least she hoped so.

"Oh you did." He wrapped his hand around her ponytail.

The gesture was possessive and pretty barbaric. She might not have believed how her body had responded to him that very first time, but nothing had changed since. He could still turn her on with little more than a glance.

"So how did you guess?" She tilted her head back, testing him. But he didn't let go of her hair. If anything his grip tightened. Was it wrong to find that so arousing?

I don't care.

"I said you managed to hide it well. I didn't say you managed to fool me."

With one hand wound around the back of his neck for support, she slid her other hand between their bodies until she came to the hard length of his erection. He pushed into her, forcing her backwards, and the backs of her thighs pressed against the edge of the desk.

"Why didn't I?" She slowly moved her hand down his length and cupped him. He made a strangled sound in his throat and pulled on her hair, forcing her head back.

"Babe, you might've been going for the don't-touch-me librarian look, but all I could see was that fuck-me-now gleam in your eyes."

Well, she had asked. And his response enchanted her. Not that she was going to let him know. "I must have picked up on your primitive sexual vibes then."

He laughed and ground his cock into her hand. "Why do you think I sat behind my desk? I couldn't risk you seeing how much I wanted you. Not when," he paused for a second and a wicked gleam entered his eyes. "*Fraternization* with clients is strictly off-limits."

"Thankfully, I'm not your client." It was crazy how re-lieved she'd been when her deposit had reappeared in her account. It was one thing to hire a bodyguard as a fake boyfriend. It was another to have wild monkey sex with him.

Obviously Jackson felt exactly the same way.

"You're definitely not my client." He clasped her ass. "But I still owe you one from that night. And I have every intention that you will collect."

She knew exactly what he was talking about.

Jackson had promised she would scream his name as he made her come. But she had the illogical conviction that once she did, for him the game would be over.

If that was true, it made him hopelessly shallow. But it didn't make any difference. She didn't want this—whatever *this* was—to end.

"What are you waiting for?" She sounded hoarse but if the way Jackson's grip on her tightened was anything to go by, he clearly thought she sounded sexy.

"Drop your jeans." It was a growled command.

"What?" She wasn't sure whether to laugh or just do as he said.

"Now."

She still had the insane urge to giggle but tugged open her jeans and pushed them over her hips. "Your turn."

His gaze raked over her. "Get rid of the thong."

His hand was still tangled in her hair, restricting her movement. She hooked her thumbs into the lacy band of her thong and slowly eased the wispy material over her thighs. She gyrated her hips for good measure.

"Anything else?" She inched her tee shirt up, giving him a fleeting glimpse of her midriff before tugging it over her stomach again. She loved the way his entire focus was centered on her, as though she was the only woman in his world.

Am I the only woman he's sleeping with? She'd never asked. She desperately wanted to be.

"Yeah. Turn around and put your hands on the desk."

She'd had visions of lying flat on her back and wrapping her legs around Jackson. *His way sounds more fun.*

"Sounds like you've done this before." She shot him a careless smile so he wouldn't guess that, yet again, this was another first for her. As she shuffled around, her jeans impeding her movement, he released his grip on her hair.

"I've never had anyone over this desk before." He sounded on the point of laughing. "I've never taken any woman over a desk before. First time for everything."

"Huh." She was relieved he couldn't see the crazy smile on her face. "That's for sure."

Before she guessed his intention, he pulled her jeans down and off her right leg, sneaker included. She looked over her shoulder to see him admiring her naked butt with a definite predatory gleam in his eyes.

I love the way he looks at me. As though he was about to devour her.

"Enjoying yourself?"

"Best view I've seen this year." He caught her gaze and grinned. "Your ass is edible. Have I ever told you that?"

Her mouth was dry. It was slightly surreal to be conducting a conversation about her ass when she was bent over his desk with said ass on display for the world to see.

Even if at this moment the world was comprised solely of Jackson.

"Once or twice."

He was very complimentary about her ass. But then he was equally appreciative of her legs and breasts. She'd never been with anyone else who was so vocal in his admiration for her body.

It was more than a little addictive.

He spread her legs with the simple tactic of pushing her foot with his boot. "How's your fantasy coming along so far?"

There was no comparison. She pressed her forehead against the desktop. "Reality beats it, hands down."

He rubbed her ass cheeks. The thought of him looking at her was as powerful a turn on as the friction warming her exposed skin and she wriggled helplessly.

She raised her head just enough that she could hitch in a ragged breath. "Aren't you forgetting something? You're still fully dressed. That's hardly fair."

"Who said anything about fair?" There was a dangerous edge in his voice. "This is your fantasy. You didn't say anything about me being naked on the desk with you."

She was pretty sure in her fantasy they were both rolling around the desk without as much as a wisp of lace between them.

His warm breath dusted her lower back, and then his teeth nipped the fleshy mound of her ass. It was shocking, unexpected, and a gurgle of pleasure spilled from her parted lips.

She closed her eyes and bit down on her knuckles before another mortifying noise could escape.

• • •

Jackson groaned as Scarlett quivered beneath him. He didn't want to rush things but she was so wet, so ready.

In the back of his mind lurked the knowledge that they could be interrupted at any moment. It was enough to propel him into action, and within nanoseconds he'd torn open his jeans and rolled on a condom.

She was splayed over his desk. In his fantasies Scarlett wore stockings and six-inch heels. But he'd never seen anything to beat the sight of her jeans crumpled around her ankles, one foot bare, and her naked ass his for the taking.

It didn't matter what she wore or where they were. He wanted her with a savage need that bordered on insanity. No other woman had ever invaded his thoughts the way Scarlett did. She was his drug of choice.

"Jackson." The way she said his name, all breathy and needy with desire, pushed him closer to the edge. "You're killing me here."

She was the one doing the killing. And he didn't have a clue how to stop her.

He slid his hands beneath her thighs, lifting her from the desk. She wriggled her hips, an irresistible invitation, and he pushed into her slick heat. Her choked gasp arrowed straight to his balls and she arched her back, taking his full length deep inside.

"You feel so fucking good." He shoved his hand under her tee. Even through her bra he could feel the hard peak of her nipple. Her sexy little moans and the way she tightened around his cock damn near splintered his reason.

His hot gaze raked along her back, where he'd wrenched up her tee shirt. The smooth skin of her hips and ass contrasted with his denim-clad legs. The sight of his dick sinking into her naked flesh, while he was fully clothed, heightened the lust pounding through his body. He slowly withdrew, savoring the way her slit contracted around him as though she didn't want to let him escape.

"Harder," she panted. He didn't need any other encouragement. He cupped her sex, pressed one finger against her sensitive clit, and slammed into her from behind.

She gasped and he pulled his hand from her breast and wound her hair around his fist. A primitive surge of possessiveness engulfed him and once again he leaned over her and growled in her ear.

"You're my woman, Scarlett." The words were out before he even knew what he was going to say.

He fucked her, hard and fast, the way she wanted, and beyond the thunder of his heartbeat he heard her throaty scream.

"Jackson."

Jackson wrapped his arms around Scarlett and held her tight. She was flat on the desk and he was sprawled on top of her. He didn't want to move—ever.

He had no idea how long they'd been in his office or how long it had been since they'd come. All he knew was that here, with Scarlett, the outside world no longer mattered.

Peace. That was the strange sensation flooding through his body. And the second he identified it, unease stirred.

Sexually satisfied was the only way he should be feeling right now. That, and a sense of needing his own space.

I don't want to let her go. Even their very first night together he'd stayed longer than he had intended. *Why was she so different from all the others?*

With damning reluctance, he pulled out of her. The air chilled him as he hastily took care of business, and Scarlett pushed herself upright and straightened her clothes.

After a few minutes, when she still hadn't said anything, he shot her a glance.

She tugged her fingers through her ponytail and avoided facing him.

Fuck. Had she read more into his fucking stupid comment than he'd meant?

What the hell had *he meant?*

"Hey, you okay?" He tugged the end of her ponytail and she turned to him. There was an odd expression on her face he couldn't name, as though she was sizing him up and wasn't sure what to make of him.

"I'm fine." She smiled but it didn't reach her eyes. "Are you?"

"Sure." His fingers tightened on her hair before he forced himself to let go. He had the uneasy feeling he should say something about his comment since it obviously loomed between them, but for the life of him he didn't have the first idea what.

Maybe he could just ignore it. He'd take Scarlett out for dinner somewhere.

If she could cancel her plans for tonight.

"Jackson." She was leaning back against his desk, her fingers curled over its edge. Despite the smile that was still on her face, she didn't look exactly relaxed. His plans for spending the rest of the day with her faded.

"Yeah?" He shoved his hands into his back pockets so he wouldn't be tempted to touch her instead. She obviously didn't want him to.

She cleared her throat and fixed her gaze on his chest. Not a good sign. "I know what we have is very, um, casual…" Her voice trailed off and she licked her lips. Fuck, what had possessed him to tell her she was his woman? Sure, his brain might have been deprived of oxygen at the time but that was no excuse to say stuff that could be misunderstood or twisted out of shape.

Except Scarlett Ashford is my woman.

He shoved the rebellious thought aside. Why the hell did he keep thinking that?

"Forget it." He forced a laugh. He hoped it sounded more natural to her than it did to himself. "I've never gone in for exclusivity. You know that."

Her smile wavered. "Yes, of course. It's just… I guess I wondered, that's all."

Was Scarlett seeing other men? Was she seeing another man this weekend? It had never even crossed his mind before. The possibility caused a hard knot in the center of his chest.

He didn't want Scarlett fucking any other man.

He'd never cared about that side of things before. This was getting too deep for him to handle. He should just walk away while he still could.

"I've been flat out at work for the last month or so, plus with the dojo…" So much for walking away.

She blinked and looked completely confused. "Oh, right."

He resisted the urge to tug at his collar. Sweat trickled along the back of his neck. It would be easier to simply ask her if she was screwing other guys but he couldn't summon up the words.

"What I'm saying is, I haven't been with other women for a while."

It hadn't even occurred to him to pick up another woman for a night of mindless sex since he'd met Scarlett. Why would he even want to?

He wasn't going to tell her that though.

"Haven't you?" She sounded surprised. No, she sounded *amazed*. He wasn't sure whether to take that as a compliment or insult. "Oh. I haven't either. Dated other men, I mean."

Relief thudded through him. He didn't even find any issue with the word *dated*. What was so bad about the word anyway? All it meant was he and Scarlett were seeing each other for sex with the occasional detour for coffee and dinner.

It worked for him.

Which reminded him. He was going to take Scarlett out for something to eat. A date, no less.

Before he managed to get his shit together and ask her, her cell rang. She sighed when she saw the caller ID.

"Sorry, I have to take this." She angled away from him. "Hey, Liv. I know. I'll be there soon. I got held up."

She smiled over her shoulder and he grinned back. He had no idea who Liv was, but it wasn't some guy Scarlett was seeing, which was all that mattered.

"Held up?" He scoffed as she tossed her cell back in her purse. "Is that what you call it?"

"Trust me, if I'd told Liv what I'd been up to, she wouldn't let me go until I'd shared every last detail."

He wrapped his arm around her shoulders and they made their way out of the dojo. Scarlett slid her fingers into his back pocket and her palm rested against his butt. It felt good. He locked up and tugged her a little closer. "You busy all weekend?"

"Why? Did you have something in mind?"

Yeah. He didn't want to wait three days before he saw

her again. "We could hang out. Grab something to eat."

He chanced giving her a sideways glance. She had the same amazed expression on her face as when he'd told her he hadn't been with anyone else. He really had no idea how to ask a woman out on a date.

"I'd love to. But things are pretty full on this weekend."

"Sure. Some other time." They reached his car, but he still had his arm around her. She didn't seem in any hurry to let go of his butt, either.

"The thing is," she tensed, as though she wasn't sure how he'd take her next comment. "Liv and I—Liv's my cousin, by the way—organize an annual charity ball to raise funds for *Rose Marie House.* And it's tomorrow night. That's why we're getting together now, to go over all the last minute details."

A charity ball. Of all the things he might have imagined her doing this weekend, this didn't even come close.

"Right." He didn't know what else to say. People he knew might give up their time to help out, or donate to favorite causes. But they didn't organize balls.

Obviously his response wasn't enough, if Scarlett's rigid body was anything to go by. And then he remembered their earlier conversation, when he'd almost bitten her head off when she'd suggested his dojo might be a charity.

Shit.

He needed to let her know he thought what she did was great. If only he could find the fucking words.

"You organized the whole thing?"

"Yes. Well, between Liv and I, we have plenty of contacts." She offered him a half smile. She still wasn't sure about his reaction.

"And you're not afraid to use them."

It was the right thing to say. She laughed and the tension drained from her as she leaned against him. "That's right. This is only the third year we've done it, but the last two years were very successful. Sometimes having the Ashford name comes in very handy."

He bet it did. But not everyone with an influential name used it the way she did. "You still put in the hard yards. Don't put yourself down, babe."

"That's… thanks, Jackson." There was a strange catch in her voice. "Sometimes people seem to think it's all a game or some kind of hobby for me. But it's not."

"What the hell do they know?" He gave her a grin, but inside he was pissed that anyone would try and devalue the work Scarlett did. "You're one in a million. Don't ever forget it."

"You're pretty special yourself." She smiled up at him, as though he'd made her day. "Don't *you* ever forget it."

Like he'd ever forget this conversation. It was the first time a woman had ever said *he* was special.

"How long does a charity ball take to organize?"

"Well, put it this way. Next month we'll start putting together next year's ball."

"Enjoy organizing events, do you?" Maybe he could ask her to help get some more publicity for saving Heyward Street. Ella had told him he needed to organize a rally or something, but he had no idea where to start with that kind of thing.

"Apparently," Scarlett said, "I have a talent for it."

He grinned and kissed her. Long and slow and damn but it was hard to pull back. "That's not your only talent, babe."

"Flattery." She shook her head in mock disgust. Then the smile slid from her face and she gave him an odd look. "Jackson."

"Yeah?" He unlocked the car but made no move to release her.

She licked her lips in a strangely nervous gesture. "You can say no. You won't hurt my feelings. But if you're not doing anything tomorrow night I'd love—I mean, it would be great if you wanted to come to the ball."

Ten minutes ago he'd wanted to ask Scarlett out to grab a pizza. Now she'd just asked him to go to a ball. Talk about a different world.

"Sure."

"You will?" It was obvious she hadn't expected him to accept. So why had she asked him?

"I've nothing else planned. I'd like to see how you put it together."

"Oh." She continued to stare at him as though she still couldn't believe he'd agreed to go to her ball. "Good. Well, I'll get you a VIP pass and let security know."

"Okay." He hid his grin as she got in the car. It wouldn't be the first time he'd gone to a high society function, but this would be the first time he'd use a VIP guest pass.

Chapter Fifteen

Jackson took a deep breath as he strode into the marble-pillared reception of the hotel. A courier had delivered an embossed invitation and security clearance to *Graysons'* that morning, as he and Scarlett had arranged the day before. He handed the card to a guard and tried to act natural. The only other times he'd been to anything like this, he'd been the one checking out the guests' IDs.

He made his way toward the ballroom. The massive double doors were open and he caught sight of the rich and famous Scarlett counted among her friends.

Just like her father's wedding, this was a different world.

"Hey, Jackson?" A deep voice pulled him back to the present. Mitch Chandler, a guy he'd met through work connections, grinned at him. If they'd been anywhere else, they would've punched each other's arms in greeting.

"Mitch. Been a while."

"Too long." Mitch glanced toward the ballroom. "Who're

you with tonight?"

"Not working tonight." Jackson resisted the urge to loosen his tie. "I'm a VIP guest." He leered smugly at Mitch, since he could imagine what the other man thought of that.

"Fuck. Who'd you kill?"

"It's all legit." He almost told Mitch who he was with but something stopped him. Scarlett might have invited him tonight but he didn't know if she wanted him telling people that.

"Undercover?" Mitch's gaze scanned the area.

He wasn't undercover, but he should have checked how physical she wanted them to be in public. He had a tough time keeping his hands off of her.

"No. See you." He made his way into the ballroom, ignoring the cocktails offered to him. A sea of white and pink greeted him, from the tables to the covered chairs, the countless displays of flowers, and the floating helium balloons.

He caught sight of Scarlett. She wore a long pink dress that sparkled every time she moved, and glittering jewelry was threaded through her hair. She was talking to a couple of high profile politicians, sleazy bastards the pair of them. Should he go over and interrupt? Or would that give them a good excuse not to dig deep into their pockets for Scarlett's charity?

When she noticed him, her smile lit up the room. Christ, he had it bad. She made her excuses to the two men before she crossed the floor to him.

Fucking gorgeous.

"Jackson." She leaned in close and kissed his cheek. Her perfume was different tonight, but it suited her as well as her usual. Subtle, addictive, and classy.

"You're beautiful." He resisted the urge to pull her close for a proper kiss.

"Am I?" She tipped her head to one side and fluttered her eyelashes at him. Did she have pink glitter on her eyelashes as well? "Well, thank you."

"Very pink." Even her nails were pink.

"It's supposed to be tea rose. Last year we went with misty rose. Next year—well, that's something Liv and I have yet to agree on."

Rose. He should've guessed, considering why this ball was being held. "This is really something, you know that?" He couldn't imagine how much work was involved in putting together something like this. Sure, Scarlett had contacts but everything still needed to be coordinated.

Maybe he would ask her for some pointers in spreading the word about saving his dojo.

"It seems to be going well so far." She glanced around the room and he saw her bite her lip. But that was the only sign she gave. Anyone looking at her would think she was completely relaxed.

He threaded his fingers through hers and tugged her a little closer.

"You got a problem you want me to sort out?"

The tension drained from her and she shook her head. "No. But thanks. It's just being on display, you know? There's no way around it tonight. The pre-publicity is no problem because Liv loves being in the limelight. So she deals with that side of things while I'm happy to do the admin stuff."

"Nothing would get done without the admin stuff."

"True." She squeezed his fingers. *Since when did holding hands feel so good?*

"Oh, you haven't got a drink." Scarlett raised one finger to a passing waiter who appeared like magic by their side. She took a flute of champagne and handed it to him. "Fine host I am."

He took the flute although he had no intention of drinking it. "You're the best. Don't let anyone tell you otherwise."

"You're so good for my ego."

"I'm just telling you the truth. There aren't many who could put something like this together. No matter how many contacts they have."

She trailed the tips of her fingers across his chest. "It's a shame my family doesn't see it that way."

What the hell was wrong with those people? "They don't see you the way I do."

Her smile damn near took his breath away. Then she gave a little sigh. "The auction's starting in a minute. Will you be okay if I just—"

"Go." He released her fingers. "I'm a big boy. I can look after myself for one night."

He watched her walk away and then prowled around the perimeter of the ballroom. Old habits died hard, and he spent most of the time sizing up all the guests.

The auction was something else. The donations on offer ranged from original artwork and exclusive hand made jewelry to a cruise to Antarctica. He stood at the back of the room, his gaze fixed on Scarlett, who was on the stage looking as though she belonged there. No one would guess how hard this side of things was for her.

"Didn't expect to see you here." The voice cut through him and he gritted his teeth. He should've known Edward Saunders would be there. "On duty, are you?"

Obviously Saunders now knew what he did for a living. "No."

Saunders noticeably stiffened by his side, and Jackson allowed a grim smile to surface. Bastard clearly hadn't expected that answer.

"Scarlett does enjoy her little charitable gestures."

The smile died. He knew damn well Saunders wasn't referring to the ball. He didn't give the other man the satisfaction of looking his way and kept his gaze on Scarlett.

"Scarlett's doing a great job."

"Of course she is. She was born to host extravagant charity events. On the other hand, from what I've heard, you're more used to being on the receiving end."

Jackson forgot about not rising to the other man's bait and swung around. Saunders smirked at him. He wanted to grind the smug bastard's face into the nearest wall.

He dredged up his years of Aikido training. He might hate thinking about that time of his life but it had happened. It was about time he owned it.

"That's right. It helped me and my brothers survive when we were kids. You got some moral objection to helping kids who live in poverty?"

A muscle twitched in Saunders's jaw. He obviously hadn't expected that response. "Don't twist my words, Grayson. We both know you don't belong here, unless you're being paid."

Of course he knew he didn't belong here. Scarlett was way out of his league, but he didn't need a prick like Saunders to rub his nose in it.

"Hey." Scarlett appeared by his side and there was something brittle about the smile she flashed between him and Saunders. He had a powerful need to sling his arm around her shoulders and show Saunders he most certainly wasn't Scarlett's pet charity project, but he'd be damned if he'd let the other man dictate anything when it came to Scarlett.

"Hey. Auction went well." At least he thought it had, if the unbelievable bids were anything to go by.

"Yes. Everyone's been so generous."

"I won the romantic weekend package in Venice," Saunders announced, giving Scarlett a slimy grin and leaving no one in any doubt who he expected to take with him. "What did you bid on, Grayson?"

Since the vast majority of bids had started in the four figure range, the answer to that was none. Jackson might no longer be poverty-stricken but he didn't have that kind of disposable cash lying around either.

Neither had he paid for his ticket. Scarlett had been horrified when he'd offered to yesterday, so he'd intended to make a donation tonight instead.

But he hadn't made the donation yet. There was no way Saunders could know any of that but it still grated.

"Jackson isn't here to bid." There was an edge in Scarlett's voice. "He doesn't just put his hand in his pocket once a year. He's on the front line."

How about that? He had the mad urge to grin at her unexpected defense but managed to give a noncommittal grunt instead.

Saunders looked pissed enough to spit, as though Scarlett had just personally insulted him. Which he guessed in a way she had.

"Shouldn't you still be up on stage, sweetheart?" Saunders said, giving her a smile a shark would be proud of. "The press is going crazy. It's not right that Livia takes all the credit."

"It's fine. She loves giving sound bites."

"It's not fine. You need to be seen. It's what the people want."

"Fuck the people," Jackson said. "Scarlett doesn't have to suck up to the press if she doesn't want to."

Saunders sniffed, the little prick. "You obviously have no idea how these things work. The Ashford name opens doors, but Scarlett, sweetheart..." He turned back to Scarlett and what the fuck was all this sweetheart shit? "You have to give them their money's worth."

Scarlett had a polite smile fixed to her face, but Jackson saw her tense as though Saunders' comment had stung.

Irritation rolled through him. "Back off." He took a step toward Saunders and only stopped when Scarlett wrapped her hand around his arm. He flung one last glare in Saunders's direction before turning to Scarlett. "You've done enough. They've gotten more than their money's worth tonight."

Her polite smile cracked into something warmer. She didn't let go of his arm. "Thanks, Jackson. And it's not as though I've been a hermit. They've got photos of me. It's just—"

"You don't need to explain yourself." He was pissed she thought she needed to explain anything, when anyone with half a brain could see how much work she'd put into tonight. He shot Saunders a deadly glare. The other man offered Scarlett a stiff smile before stalking off.

Scarlett squeezed his arm. She looked as though she was trying not to laugh. "I'll introduce you to Liv when she's finished wrapping the press around her little finger. She's dying to meet you."

It was after three when the final guests left. Jackson pulled Scarlett against him. "You done here?"

"Just about." Then she straightened. "Oh wait. I need to give the pink diamonds back."

He watched as a couple of burly bodyguards he'd seen throughout the night approached. Scarlett and Liv helped each other pull the strings of diamonds from their hair before handing them to the silent men.

"You hired your jewelry?"

"Honey, why hire it when they're happy to loan it?" Liv said. "Anyway, I'm for bed. If I didn't know Scarlett would claw my eyes out, I'd invite you along for the ride, Jackson." She fluttered her eyelashes at him while Scarlett slapped her arm.

He laughed. Liv was fun but she sure wasn't Scarlett. He liked the fact that she had obviously told her cousin about them. Sure, she'd introduced him as her friend, and it was obvious Liv thought *friends with benefits*.

He could deal with that.

"Do you need a ride home?" The security detail was hanging about but it didn't feel right leaving Scarlett.

"Well, I was going to crash at Liv's tonight."

"Hon, even I'm not that much of a bitch to deprive you of a night with your Jackson." Liv clutched Scarlett's arm and then whispered loud enough for him to hear. "Just make sure you tell me every detail tomorrow."

Liv left. Scarlett looked as though she wasn't sure whether she should follow her cousin or not. It was kind of awkward. He'd never been to Scarlett's place and he'd never invited her back to his.

Before she could run, he caught her hand. "Stay with me tonight."

. . .

Scarlett stirred. Something wasn't quite right. She forced open one eye and blurred, unfamiliar objects slowly came into focus. Shock stabbed through her, jerking her fully awake.

She'd stayed last night at Jackson's.

He'd never invited her to his home before. And the first time he did, she'd been so exhausted all she'd done was fall asleep.

Before she could obsess about that, the bedroom door swung open and Jackson strolled into the room. She sat up and dragged a hand through her hair. She hadn't cleaned her face last night or brushed her teeth. She slapped her hand across her mouth in horror. Not only did she look a fright, she had morning breath as well.

Jackson, of course, was gorgeous. He was also holding take out coffee and a bakery box.

Her stomach grumbled. *Ugh. How sexy is that?*

"Morning, babe." He grinned, apparently not caring about her appearance or noisy stomach. She sagged against the pillows and yawned. "My shirt looks a lot better on you than it does me."

"Mm." She stretched and yawned again. What time was it? Definitely still the morning. No wonder she could hardly keep her eyes open. "I'm surprised you didn't tear it off me in the night and have your wicked way."

He laughed and sat next to her on the bed. "It crossed my mind. A few times." He handed her a coffee. "But you looked so cute asleep. Plus I don't think you could've stayed awake long enough to do anything."

Considering it had been almost four-thirty before they'd arrived at Jackson's place, he was probably right. *Wouldn't have minded him trying, though.* She took a long swallow of coffee. "That's so good."

He opened the box to an assortment of freshly baked pastries and pulled her against him. She sighed and snuggled into his warmth. She could get so used to this.

Somehow this seemed like a really big deal, as though they'd moved onto another level of their relationship.

Maybe she was just fooling herself. But he'd gone to her ball and hadn't cared if people assumed they were together.

She might've fallen for Jackson against all her best intentions. But maybe it wouldn't end with her getting her heart broken. If she gave him enough time he'd see they had so much more than whatever he thought *this* was.

"This is kind of strange."

"What is?" She helped herself to an almond croissant. It was light and warm and she'd never tasted anything so perfect. Or maybe that had something to do with the company.

"This." Jackson waved his coffee in the general direction of the baked goods. "Breakfast in bed. Is this a date?"

She choked on her croissant. Had he really just said the *D* word? She hadn't expected him to leap to that conclusion so soon. It had to be a sign that she wasn't the only one who thought they could have a future together.

"I don't know. I've never had a breakfast date before so

I guess it can be, if you want."

"Okay." That's all he said, but it was enough. She took another sip of coffee and tried not to obsess over a simple four-letter word.

But she couldn't help it.

She wanted Jackson in every aspect of her life. Not just for hot sex. She wanted to show him off and let everyone know that he was *hers*.

There was one sure way of doing that. To invite him to an Ashford family party, where only close relatives and official partners were welcome. The Fourth of July party her dad gave would be the perfect opportunity.

Something had definitely shifted. Even her stupid fear that he'd be finished with her after she screamed his name during sex had finally disappeared.

She could agonize over it all morning. There was only one way to find out for sure whether he was ready to face her family now that he was no longer only her fake date.

• • •

Jackson gave Scarlett a sideways glance. He liked having her in his bed, sharing breakfast. He wouldn't mind doing it more often. *How the hell do I tell her something like that?*

"Do you have anything planned for the fourth?" Scarlett licked some stray flakes of pastry from the corner of her mouth with the tip of her tongue.

She has no idea how sexy she is.

It took him a couple of seconds to focus on what she'd just asked him.

The only plan he had for the holiday was the usual

afternoon trip with his brothers to visit their gran. It had become an unspoken tradition. But he sure as hell was free if she wanted to do something in the evening.

"Why?"

"Oh, it's nothing really." She brushed a few crumbs off his shirt. "But my dad's back from his honeymoon next week and we're having this welcome home party. I thought if you were free you might like to come along."

Being invited to lavish Ashford functions was starting to become a habit. While he had no great urge to spend any more time with the same crowd who'd been at the wedding, he did want to spend the time with Scarlett.

"Sure." It was hard to maintain his sense of cool when Scarlett gave him one of her gorgeous smiles. "What time?"

"The barbecue starts about four, so anytime before then would be great. Say about three?"

That fucking sucked. It didn't matter what he did now, he was screwed. That was the exact time he and his brothers were due at their gran's.

Chapter Sixteen

A few nights later, Jackson walked into *Murphy's* and scanned the crowded pub for his brothers. They'd made this their local hangout several years ago, an unspoken tribute to their mother's Irish ancestry. Not that Jackson really remembered his mother. She'd died when he was eight.

He remembered the god-awful rows between her and his father, though. And the violence. Nothing had ever been proven, but he and his brothers knew in their gut that her life with their brutal father had killed her.

That fucking bastard. Jackson's chest tightened as the memories clawed through his mind. He shoved them away. His father wasn't worth getting riled up over. Not now. He, Alex, and Cooper had moved on from their past. And while they might have all flouted the law and played with fire as teens, thank God for their gran's steady presence in their lives.

She was their rock. And once their father was out of

their lives she'd laid down the law all right. She might have been as poor as dirt but she made sure they all treated her like a lady.

They might've earned money illegally and treated her to luxury items they'd traded on the black market. She was fine with that. But they all knew where she drew the line. And that line was no man ever raised his hand in anger against a woman.

She'd suffered watching her daughter tied to a man with no backbone. But she'd made it clear her grandsons weren't following him down that path.

As if she'd needed to tell them that. None of them had ever wanted to follow their father anywhere.

He caught sight of Cooper slouched over a table in the corner and made his way over. "Alex not here yet?"

"Nah." There was a weird note in Cooper's voice as he read a text on his cell.

Jackson dragged his mind away from Scarlett and the Ashford party in a couple of days to frown at his brother. "Trouble?"

"It's just Scott."

Cooper and Scott had been friends forever, and Scott's baby sister had hit it big on some soap a few years back. Jackson had no idea why a message from Scott would distract Cooper. "Is he okay?"

Cooper turned his cell off and tossed it onto the table. "Yeah." He picked up his beer and took a long swallow from the bottle. When it became obvious that line of conversation had died, Jackson made his way to the bar to get himself a beer. He ordered a second when he saw Alex pushing his way through the crowd.

This was going to be fun. He'd already spoken to their gran and been secretly taken aback at how okay she'd been about his change of plans for the fourth. Then she'd completely shocked him by suggesting he bring Scarlett to visit her sometime.

Like that would ever happen. Only problem was, he hadn't been able to get the idea out of his head since. He had the weirdest feeling the two women would get on well, despite their wildly differing backgrounds.

He handed Alex his beer and they sat opposite each other, either side of Cooper. As Jackson took a swig, he thought how symbolic that was. Cooper, despite being the youngest brother, was often the buffer between him and Alex.

"About tomorrow," Alex said. "I've asked Ella to join us."

Jackson choked on his beer. Had his big bro finally seen the light there?

"Ella always spends the holiday with her mom." Cooper slung Jackson a look that clearly conveyed they were on the same wavelength when it came to Alex and Ella.

Alex frowned. "I know. That's why her mom is coming along too."

"Are you fucking mad?" Cooper said. "Ella's mom drives gran up the wall."

"I've cleared it with her," Alex said. "She's fine if it means Ella will turn up. It'll give you a chance to spend some time with her, Cooper. She was saying the other day she's hardly seen you in weeks."

Cooper grunted in a noncommittal manner. Jackson mentally rolled his eyes and finished his beer. Alex wasn't just blind when it came to Ella. He was also completely delusional if he thought she was interested in Cooper in that way.

Jackson might as well get it over with. "I can't make it to gran's."

"What do you mean, you can't make it?" Alex placed his beer back on the table.

"I mean I can't make it."

"It's just for a couple of hours, Jackson. Reschedule your other appointment."

Not happening, unless he didn't turn up at the Ashford's until after six. "No."

"Doesn't sound work related to me." Cooper leered at him over his beer. "Sounds like your dick leading you astray again, J."

Jackson ignored his brother's remarks. Alex, on the other hand, shot Cooper a sharp glance before refocusing on Jackson.

"You still seeing that Ashford girl?"

Alex looked perfectly relaxed, except for the flicker of emotion in his eyes. And it wasn't anywhere near the juvenile mockery Cooper tended to display.

"What if I am?"

"Thought you decided to finish things with her."

I never said that. It irritated the shit out of him that his brother thought he had the right to dictate his affairs.

But mixed in with the irritation, the old guilt surfaced. Guilt that Alex had taken the fall for him twelve years ago. Guilt that he, Jackson, hadn't been strong enough to stand up to their father for both himself and Cooper.

It was the reason he couldn't—wouldn't—tell Alex to fuck off and mind his own business. Because Alex had sacrificed too much in the past trying to protect him and Cooper.

"No." That was all he said. That was all he needed to say, because it said it all.

The following morning he'd just stepped out of the shower when the doorbell rang. It was only six. Who the hell turned up on a person's doorstep at six in the morning?

With a muttered curse, he pulled on a pair of jeans and slung a towel over his shoulder before he went downstairs. He'd bought the house a couple of years ago and while it was a long way from the refined estates Scarlett was used to, the neighborhood was far less bloody than the one he'd grown up in.

He pulled open the door...and was confronted by two burly goons in black suits.

"Jackson Grayson?" said the one on the left, but Jackson wasn't fooled. They knew exactly who he was. As did the man sitting in the back of the sleek black limo parked on the road outside.

"That's right." Jackson looked back at the speaker. If pushed he was sure he could take on the pair of them and come out on top.

"This way." The goon swept his arm in the direction of the car. "Mr. Ashford would like a word with you."

Jackson knew what that meant. At least he knew what it meant in his world. Maybe it didn't necessarily mean getting the shit kicked out of you in the world of the Ashford's.

He wouldn't bet on it though.

He grabbed his keys from the side table and sauntered toward the limo. One of Ashford's thugs opened the door for him, and Jackson took a deep breath and got in.

The scent of leather and polished wood assaulted him. There would be no covert knife in the ribs here. It would ruin the upholstery.

"Thank you for agreeing to see me." Ashford gave him a cold smile. Scarlett obviously got her looks from her mother because Jackson could see nothing of her in this man.

"Sure." *Like I had a choice.* If Ashford thought he could intimidate Jackson with his flashy car and second-rate body-guards, he was mistaken.

He waited for the other man to finish with his probing look, which was clearly designed to unnerve him. *Not going to happen.* He just wished Ashford would get on with the threats and get it over with. What would his angle be? *Stay away from my daughter if you don't want a couple of broken legs?*

It would take more than a few broken bones to keep him from seeing Scarlett.

"I understand my daughter has invited you to the party tomorrow."

Jackson didn't bother to respond. Ashford flicked non-existent dirt from his suit pants, and for a second, the gesture reminded Jackson of Scarlett.

"I suggest you tell her you're unable to attend."

Irritation flared through him, even though he'd known the demand was coming. "Why would I do that?"

"Because I can make it worth your while to stay away from Scarlett for good. Name your price."

For a second he stared at Ashford in disbelief. Did he

seriously think he could buy him off simply by writing a fucking check?

"I don't want your money." He ground the words between his teeth. *You can shove your fucking money up your—*

"Scarlett has the Ashford name, but she wields no power. You'll get nowhere if you insist on continuing this... liaison."

Don't fucking lose it. "I'm not with Scarlett because of her name."

Jackson's hands were fisted, and he forcibly relaxed his muscles. If Ashford's intention was to make him lose his cool, he was well on the way to achieving his goal.

Don't give him the satisfaction. He exhaled a long breath and flattened his palms against his thighs. It wasn't the thought of being mashed to a pulp by the men in black if he smashed his fist into Ashford's smug face. It was not being able to look Scarlett in the eyes again if he raised his hand against her father.

"I gather you're opposed to some redevelopment work that's being proposed in Heyward Street."

"*What?*"

Ashford gave another of his cold smiles. "I can make it go away, Grayson. Permanently."

Ashford's words acted like an icy shower. Jackson leaned across the space between them, until his face was just inches from Ashford's.

"I don't need your help to make my problems go away." His voice reminded him of his brother Alex. "And I'll tell you this for nothing, Ashford. It disgusts me that you think you can use Scarlett in this way to get what you want."

He turned and got out of the car. Then he looked back at Ashford. For a second the mask slipped, and the hint of a smirk touched Ashford's lips.

It was enough to crack Jackson's icy calm, and again he had the suicidal urge to resort to the violence that had once ruled his life. *I am not my fucking father.* He didn't need to use his fists to settle a debate.

Jackson strangled the rage and offered him a mirthless grin.

"See you tomorrow, Mr. Ashford."

Chapter Seventeen

Scarlett surreptitiously checked her watch again. It was almost four. Hadn't Jackson agreed to turn up at three? She couldn't remember now. Maybe she had just suggested he arrive at three. But the barbeque was about to start and she had the mad urge to text him to find out where he was.

She managed to resist. He'd said he was coming, and he would.

"More champagne, Scarlett?" Edward thrust a flute in her face and she backed up, irrationally annoyed that he'd interrupted her thoughts. "Your father thought you looked a little pensive over here on your own. I told him I'd take care of you."

Edward smiled in that way he had that made her want to slap his face. She wondered how her family and her dad in particular would react if she ever did such a thing.

"I don't need taking care of." She gave him a perfunctory smile, and good manners forced her to take the flute of champagne from him. What the hell was he even doing here today?

Edward laughed, as though she had said something amusing, and brushed a curl back from her face, his finger lingering on her cheek. She tilted her head away from him and took a sip of champagne.

Fuck off, asshole. If only she had the nerve to say that to his face.

"Of course you do," Edward said, oblivious to her subtle signs that she didn't want him anywhere near her. "You need a real man in your life, not a steroid enhanced goon."

Scarlett gripped the Waterford crystal stem so tightly it was a miracle the glass didn't shatter. She didn't know which part of Edward's statement to take issue with first. His pompous presumption that he was a *real man* or the dismissive dig at Jackson.

Who most certainly didn't need steroids to enhance any part of his body. The more she thought about it, the more pissed off she got.

"Jackson," she said with quiet dignity, "is not a goon, Edward, and I don't like you speaking about him in that way."

Edward gave an unconvincing show of looking astonished. "Are you still seeing him? Your father's under the impression you've split up."

They hadn't spoken about Jackson since the wedding, but he'd know Jackson was invited today. It didn't make sense her dad would think they'd split up.

Edward, you are such a jerk face. What would he do if she said *that* out loud?

And then she saw Jackson strolling across the lawn toward her. Her heart gave a strange little leap against her ribs, and warmth seeped through her chest. It was ridiculous and completely magical and she didn't care if Edward saw her besotted smile.

"Hey, babe." His sexy drawl as he reached her side caused delicious shivers across her skin. "Haven't missed anything, have I?"

"Of course not." She resisted the urge to fling her arms around his neck and eat him in full view of her entire family. Instead she gave him a demure kiss on the lips. "Now you're here, it's only just getting started."

Jackson slid his arm around her waist. Then he focused on Edward, who looked as though he'd just chewed on a chili.

"You want something?" Jackson's voice was even but Scarlett caught an undercurrent of something deadly in his tone. She frowned up at him, but he appeared to be waiting for Edward's response.

"Actually," Edward said, but Jackson interrupted him.

"*Actually,* I'm not interested in what you want." He turned to Scarlett. "I need a drink."

"Sure." She wound her arm around him and led him toward the bar beside the pool. Why couldn't she so succinctly tell Edward where to go? Jackson had once told her she was too nice. She'd been insulted at the time, but now she could see his point.

People like Edward didn't take subtle hints and polite rejections. Even her little dig at him at the ball hadn't dented his ego. He needed to be told how things stood in no uncertain terms.

Well, she'd had enough of him pawing her every time they met. If he didn't get the message today and leave her alone, she'd have no alternative but to contact him tomorrow and tell him straight.

She watched Jackson take a beer. He tipped back his head and took a long swallow. She licked her lips. He turned the simple act of drinking into an art form.

He wiped his mouth with the back of his hand and sighed. In that fleeting moment a strange look of vulnerability flashed over his face.

He seemed so tough. Except sometimes, such as now, and when he'd opened up to her at his dojo, she glimpsed another side of him. A side he had buried long ago as an act of self-preservation. She stifled the urge to wrap her arms around him and hold him close. He would never want her to see beneath the mask he showed the world.

But maybe one day he would. She hoped.

"Everything okay?" She kept her voice deliberately light as she watched him rake his gaze over the back garden.

He looked at her. She tried not to melt beneath his brooding gaze but it was hard. She took another sip of champagne to cool herself down.

"I thought it was going to be a big Ashford celebration."

A horrible thought struck her. If he'd known it was only going to be close family, wouldn't he have agreed to come? She'd been so sure their breakfast in bed had marked a milestone in their relationship. But had it all been in her head? Had she read way too much into Jackson's casual comment? She forced a laugh and shook her head.

"It's just a casual get together, that's all."

She watched him eye an immaculately turned out waiter glide by with a tray of more champagne. A chill inched over her arms as she saw the scene through his eyes.

For her family this was a casual thing. But there was still staff in the background making sure everything ran like clockwork, and the champagne was vintage.

Once again he looked at her. This time she had no desire to melt into a puddle over his boots. Instead she had the urgent wish that she had never invited him here today. That she had suggested they go somewhere, *anywhere*, else to celebrate. Just the two of them.

"This isn't my world, Scarlett." His voice was low, and she shivered at how his words so closely mirrored her own frantic thoughts. "These aren't my kind of people."

Had he turned up simply to tell her they were finished?

He couldn't do that to her. Especially not today. She'd never be able to think of Independence Day again without remembering Jackson Grayson and his own bid for freedom.

She cleared her throat. Her heart raced, making it hard to breathe properly, and the sound of the band playing in the mock-Gothic ruin folly faded to a muted buzz.

If he wanted to end whatever this was between them, he'd have to do better than pretend it was because of her family. He would have to come right out and say exactly what was on his mind.

"Your kind of people?" She drew on the years she had spent at boarding school, when all she'd wanted to do was weep for the loss of her beloved mom. But instead she'd buried it all inside and learned to hide behind a masquerade of polite smiles and perfect manners. "Care to elaborate, Jackson?"

She didn't know what she had expected him to do in response. But she certainly hadn't expected him to thread his fingers through hers and tug her close.

"None of this"—the eloquent glance around the garden told her what he meant by *this*—"is real to me, babe. When I was a kid, some nights me and my brothers went without dinner because our father had drunk away all the money."

She didn't know what to say. She squeezed his fingers and pressed their entwined hands against her heart.

He didn't say anything for a few moments, just looked at her as though he was memorizing every feature. Then, his thumb still gripping the neck of his beer bottle, he traced his finger along her cheek.

She leaned into his touch. It was crazy and bizarre, but here in the midst of her family, Jackson was opening up to her in a way he never had before, in all the times they'd been alone together.

"He didn't give a shit about any of us." There was no bitterness in his voice. He was simply stating a fact and her heart ached for the child he had been. "Not the way your dad looks out for you."

She knew her dad looked out for her. But for the last ten years, resentment against him for abandoning her at boarding school had warred with her love. And now she was so filled with guilt at her tangled feelings toward him that he was almost a stranger to her.

Any complaint she secretly nursed against him sounded petty when compared to what Jackson had just told her of his childhood.

But she had to share something of herself with him, the way he had with her.

"I know I've been lucky. But my dad and I... we haven't been close for years. Sometimes I feel that when my mom died he just stopped loving me."

I didn't just say that. It was too personal, too raw to share with anyone.

But Jackson wasn't just anyone. And he hadn't laughed in disbelief or rolled his eyes the way she always imagined anyone would if she ever confessed her secret heartache.

The brooding expression was back on his face. "People can have strange ways of showing how they feel."

"I suppose." But what wouldn't she give to have her dad look at her the way he had before her mom had died. "I'm sorry. You don't want to hear about my stupid hang-ups, not when—"

"Hey." He cut her off by tracing his finger across her lips. It was a strangely tender gesture. "Sure I do. But don't beat yourself up over it, Scarlett. You can't change the past, no matter how much you want to."

Scarlett knew it was impossible to change the past. And she loved that Jackson wanted to know about her hang-ups. But most of all she was touched by the way he was so willing to open the door on his own past.

"Is there something you wish you could change if you could?"

He gave her a grin that dissolved her good sense and handed his empty beer bottle to a passing waiter. To hell with her family. As soon as she could, she'd make their excuses and take Jackson back to her apartment.

"Yeah. I'd change having a knife stuck between my ribs for a start."

She could hardly imagine what he'd suffered. And he hadn't only been attacked with a knife. "Were you mugged?"

"No." There was no hint of amusement in his voice anymore. "I was a street fighter for four years. The money I earned helped us survive back then."

Her stomach pitched with nerves at the thought of him fighting on the streets. It was crazy to feel so sick. He was no longer living that life.

"That was pretty—" She cut herself off before she finished. It was in his past. *He hadn't died.*

"Illegal?" There was a mocking note in his tone now, and she frowned at him, ridiculously annoyed that he found it all such a joke.

"No, *dangerous* was the word that sprang to mind."

His grin faded and for a moment he looked kind of stunned by her remark. What was the matter with him? Didn't he think she'd care about his reckless behavior, just because it happened to be in the past?

"It was the only thing I could do at the time."

"What, try and get yourself killed?"

He frowned at her, but not in a pissed off way. He looked as though the fact she was concerned was a revelation to him.

"After what happened to Cooper it was a case of kill or be killed. Not literally," he added with another frown.

She knew his younger brother was Cooper but she had no idea what Jackson was talking about. Although she hadn't met him, he was definitely not dead.

"What do you mean? What happened?"

His body tensed and she clung on tighter to his hand. Just to let him know she wasn't going to let him get away that easily. Finally Jackson sighed and some of the tension seeped from him.

"Our dad was pissed out of his head one night. Used Cooper as a punching bag. If I'd known how to fall, I wouldn't have cracked my head open when that old bastard lashed out at me. *I* could've saved Cooper that night instead of laying there leaking all over the floor."

Leaking all over the floor? God, had she got it horribly wrong? Had his father killed Cooper that night?

"Saved him?" Her voice cracked. "Did your father — is Cooper dead?"

Jackson's jaw tensed. "No, he isn't, no thanks to me."

Relief flooded through her. And then his words penetrated and she frowned. "You weren't the one attacking him, Jackson. And by the sound of it you were badly injured. How could you expect to save your brother if you were all but unconscious?"

"You don't understand. Cooper was only twelve. It was my job to make sure he was okay."

"And how old were you?" He couldn't have been much older. Talk about misplaced guilt.

He stared at her as though her question made no sense. "Fourteen. Old enough."

He really did blame himself for what had happened to his brother. She wanted to hug him close and tell him he was an idiot for thinking such a thing. But that wouldn't help. He needed to work through this for himself.

"Can you tell me what happened that night?"

"Christ, what more do you need to know?" He made to pull away but she wasn't having that. Not that he tried very hard. "Cooper's always had a mouth on him. So the old man lays into him. By the time I got downstairs I thought I was too late."

Scarlett bit her lip. Although she'd had some training regarding domestic abuse, she wasn't a counselor. All she had to go on were her feelings for Jackson. She knew the kind of guy he was. He was big and he could be brash. But at his core he had a sense of honor. He wouldn't have left his brother at the mercy of their brutal father.

He had already told her as much. Yet somehow Jackson couldn't see it.

She took a deep breath. "So you left the house."

"Of course I didn't leave the house." He sounded incredulous that she could even think such a thing. But then, she didn't think that at all. "I took a swing at him. Knocked him off balance but I didn't follow through the advantage."

"Because he was your dad."

"No, that's not—" Jackson bit off his words and for a second confusion flashed over his face. "I hesitated, all right. And that's when he knocked me out."

"Because you tried to save your brother."

He didn't answer her. Had she pushed him too far?

Finally he exhaled a measured breath. "Yeah. I tried to save him. But it was Alex who saved him in the end. Cooper and me both ended up in the ER. Fine brother I was." But he offered her a cynical half smile, which was, at least, an improvement on the bitterness that had threaded through his voice up until now.

"Well, I think Cooper's very lucky to have you as his brother." She smiled up at him and he shook his head before giving a short laugh.

"Tell him that, would you? I'd like to see the look on his face."

"Oh, don't worry. I will."

His grin faded. "I've left that life behind me, Scarlett. You know that, don't you?"

"The street fighting? Yes, I know." And now she knew why he was so dedicated to saving his dojo. It wasn't just a place where kids learned martial arts. It was a refuge for those who needed it, and a symbol to Jackson that he had moved on.

His dedication to Aikido showed her that.

"Not just the street fighting." He flexed his fingers. "I don't use my fists to settle arguments any more."

A bittersweet pain pierced her heart. "I never thought you did."

He didn't say anything for a while and they simply stood, hand in hand. It might be nothing more than her imagination, but it seemed, in this moment, there was another subtle shift in their relationship.

A slow grin curved his lips. "Do you know what I want to do when you look at me like that?"

She went onto her toes and whispered in his ear. "I have a good idea."

"Failing that, I have something for you."

She rocked back onto her heels. "For me?"

For answer he pulled a crumpled envelope from his pocket. "Here. I've been meaning to give that to you for weeks."

Intrigued she handed him her flute and opened the envelope.

And pulled out her check.

Disappointment flooded through her. For a few crazy seconds there she had imagined Jackson had given her... well, she'd had no idea what he might have given her. But it hadn't been something as prosaic as returning her check.

"Ah." She pasted on a bright smile and hastily shoved

the check back into the envelope before anyone saw it. "Thanks. You could have just torn it up and thrown it away though."

Jackson placed her flute onto the tray of another passing waiter. "There's, uh, something else in there."

"Is there?" Scarlett couldn't figure out the odd expression on Jackson's face. He looked as though he was fighting the urge to snatch the envelope back from her.

She opened the envelope and peered inside. Behind the check was a small piece of card.

How weird.

She pulled it out. It was a handwritten invitation for afternoon tea the next Sunday and signed *Alice Flanagan*.

"It's from my gran." Jackson took the card from her. *Oh my God. He's embarrassed.* She stifled a giggle at the thought that Jackson's gran had the power to embarrass him. "She's decided she wants to meet you."

He made it sound like a challenge. She plucked the card from his fingers and read it again. There was no way Jackson would have passed the invite on to her if he didn't want her to meet his gran.

This was a big step.

She could play it cool. Or she could tell him the truth.

To hell with playing games. "I'd love to meet your gran."

He tried to hide it, but she saw the relief in his eyes and her heart melted into a gooey mess. Big, tough Jackson Grayson loved his gran. And he wanted them to meet.

"I'd better warn you. She's got a tough rep in our old neighborhood. But once you get to know her she's okay."

He's worried his gran might upset me. How adorable was that? "Any idea what she'd like as a thank you gift?" At his blank expression she added, "For inviting me to tea."

"I reckon putting up with me is thanks enough."

He said the best things. How long before they could leave? She couldn't wait to get him alone.

He leaned in close. "You better stop looking at me like that, Scarlett."

His breath against her ear was warm and sexy. She ran her finger over his hard bicep. "I don't want to."

He growled. God, that was hot. "I'm going to make you pay for that later."

"Oh yes?" *Please.* "How're you going to do that?"

"On your knees…"

She clutched his arm before her knees gave way. "In your dreams." *And mine.*

"You'll be begging for it."

It was hard not to beg for it *right now*. "You're a very bad man, Jackson Grayson."

His grin stole whatever was left of her heart. "It's going to be a very long evening."

Wasn't that the truth? Her panties were already damp.

She didn't want to wait hours. Heart pounding at her daring, she glanced around, but all the curious looks she and Jackson had gotten after he'd arrived had long subsided.

She gripped his hand and pulled him with her in the direction of the house.

"What're you doing?" There was a note of laughter in his voice.

"Wait and see."

Chapter Eighteen

Scarlett yanked him into a marble tiled bathroom.

She turned around and leaned against the door. In her designer dress and diamonds, she was so out of his league it hurt. But she'd brought him in here. It wasn't hard to guess why. He pulled her into his arms and did what he'd wanted to do from the minute he'd seen her standing next to Saunders.

He kissed her. Properly. Until she dug her fingers through his hair, and made those sexy little sounds that drove him insane.

Her dress was silky beneath his hands and he tugged the material up so he could grasp her naked thighs. She pulled back, gasping, and pressed her hand against his chest.

"Not so fast."

"How long do you think we've got until you're missed?" Not that he cared if anyone noticed. But Scarlett didn't like drawing attention to herself. And if they were discovered in her father's bathroom, he had the feeling the gossip would mortify her.

"I don't know. But I need to lock the other door first." She slid from his grasp and went to lock the door that, presumably, led directly into the house itself. Then she turned and gave him a look that promised this was going to be one barbeque he wouldn't forget in a hurry.

"Get your ass over here." It was a growled command as he undid his belt.

"Good things come to those who wait."

"We don't have time to wait." If someone banged on the door right now he'd fucking explode.

She smiled and slowly tugged a thick cream and gold towel from a rail, before sauntering across the room toward him, the towel dragging on the floor behind her. It was kind of unreal.

"I like my comforts," she said as she folded it up before dropping it at his feet. Then she wound her arms around his neck and nibbled kisses along his jaw until she reached his ear. "Happy Fourth of July, Jackson."

He grunted and grasped her ass, hauling her against him so she could feel how happy he was already. She gave a muffled giggle and wriggled in his arms.

"Did you just bring me in here to torture me?" *Not that I'm complaining.* If she wanted to prolong the agony until they were alone tonight he'd play the game.

"You tell me. Is this torture?" She slid down his body until she knelt on the towel at his feet. He stared at her, his mouth dry and heart pounding. Was she going down on him? *Here?*

When she tugged on his zipper he slammed his hand over hers. "Christ, Scarlett. I've dreamed about having you on your knees sucking my cock, but not in your dad's house."

She licked her lips, taking her sweet time about it, and looked up at him through her lashes in a way that made him groan.

"If you want me to stop, just say the word." She popped his button and the relief was overpowering. "I don't think you want me to, do you?" She grasped his length, and he wrapped his hand around hers, increasing the pressure. "But I wouldn't want to do anything that makes you uncomfortable."

Despite his discomfiture, he laughed. "Liar. You love it."

Her smile told him just how much she loved it. She dipped her head and the tip of her tongue swirled around the swollen head of his dick. He gritted his teeth and speared his fingers through her hair, holding her head as he pushed deep into her wet mouth. Primal lust surged through him at the sight of her on her knees, at the way her blonde hair contrasted with the black denim of his jeans.

In his fantasies Scarlett was naked as she took him into her mouth. But it didn't matter that she was fully dressed. Because her mouth was driving him to the edge of reason.

He tangled his fingers in her hair and pulled her back. Her teeth grazed his length and she looked up at him.

Fuck. He damn near lost his load right then. "Need a condom."

She lifted her mouth from him. Her lips were all pouty. "It's okay. I want to do it this way."

This was the best fucking Fourth of July he'd ever had. It was hard to think straight. "Babe, I'm clean. I've never had unprotected sex." Not even as a reckless teen.

"Nor have I." She gazed up at him. "But I've never done

this before."

It took him a heartbeat for her words to penetrate his lust soaked brain. And then his fingers involuntarily gripped her hair, holding her immobile, as he stared into her eyes.

A virgin mouth-fuck. This woman would kill him.

She roughly tugged his pants down his thighs and once again fastened her lips around him. He had to stop himself from gripping her head and forcing his length down her throat.

Her cheeks hollowed from effort as she sucked on him and he stared at her, riveted by the sight, even as his body shook with the effort not to come too soon. He wanted to prolong this moment as long as he could. But when she cupped his balls with one hand and tightened her grip around his root with her other, his willpower splintered.

He tried to pull out. She sucked harder. "Scarlett." He didn't recognize his voice. "I'm going to come."

She still didn't let go. "Babe." He tugged her hair. "You have to let me go." *Don't ever let me go.* "Can't hold on any longer."

She stroked him with her fingers. She didn't pull back. *Does she want me to come in her mouth?*

It pushed him over the edge. He pumped into her, long and hard and hot. His vision blurred and all he could see was Scarlett on her knees, taking everything he had. He clenched his teeth and tangled her hair around his fingers. And fucked her sweet mouth until he had nothing left to give.

Shuddering, he clung onto her head for a few dizzying moments until he realized she was trying to lift her face. He grabbed a hand towel from the marble topped vanity and sank to his knees before her.

"Here." His voice shook. Shit. He hoped she hadn't noticed. *But why did he hope that?* She had to know how she affected him. Without waiting for her to take it he gently wiped her mouth with the towel. She coughed, blushed, and pressed the towel to her mouth.

Transfixed, he watched her clean herself. He'd had countless blowjobs in the past. But he couldn't remember any of them.

He'd never forget this one.

But they weren't finished yet.

"Touch yourself." His voice was hoarse.

She stared at him, disbelief replacing the glazed look in her eyes. "I can't do that." She sounded faintly shocked by the notion.

"Do it for me." If he touched her, God help them both. There was no chance she'd leave this bathroom without looking as though she had been taken every which way.

Kneeling on the floor, their knees almost touched as her hand disappeared beneath her dress. That was no good. He hiked her dress up and watched her slide her hand inside her insanely sexy thong. The musky scent of her arousal filled his head, blocking out everything but the gorgeous woman in front of him.

"Stroke your clit," he ordered. Had she never touched herself this way before? It should be physically impossible, but his body hardened at the idea and he swallowed the groan that razed his throat. He didn't know why it was such a turn on, knowing she had never done this before. But it was.

Her eyes became unfocused and breathing erratic. He was caught between watching her expressive face, and the way her finger moved beneath the flimsy wisp of lace.

He ached to go down on her. To taste her as she came inside his mouth. Instead he trailed his hand along her back and cupped her rounded ass.

A shudder rippled through her and with a growl of possession he pulled her tight against his body. She bucked against him, biting his shoulder to stifle her gasps of pleasure as her orgasm claimed her.

He lost track of how long he knelt there, holding her. He never wanted to let her go. Here in her arms was the only place he wanted to be.

He closed his eyes and breathed in her familiar scent. He was still a little freaked by how much he wanted her, but it was a distant feeling. This had never happened to him before.

I've fallen for Scarlett Ashford.

Only when she lifted her head from his shoulder did he relax his hold on her. He grinned into her flushed face and she blinked back at him through mascara-smudged eyes. He'd never seen anything so fucking adorable before.

"You okay?" He brushed a damp strand of hair back from her face.

"I'm not sure. I might have died and gone to heaven."

He leaned his forehead against hers. "That's my line, babe."

She let out a ragged breath. "You're amazing, Jackson. I'd love to stay here all afternoon with you. But I guess we'd better show a face at the barbeque."

"Sure." No one had ever called him amazing before. He pulled her to her feet and watched her have a minor panic attack when she caught sight of herself in the huge wall mirror. As she rinsed out her mouth and washed her hands, he shoved his dick back into his pants and then ran his fingers through his hair. "You ready?"

She pulled an agonized face at him in the mirror and began to fluff up her hair.

"Seriously, Scarlett, you're beautiful. You don't look as though you've been up to anything, trust me."

Unlike his comment after the first time they'd had sex, this time he actually meant to reassure her. By the way she bit her lip, it was obvious she wasn't convinced.

He wrapped his arms around her as she examined every inch of her face and neck for any signs of what they'd just been up to. After a few moments her tense muscles relaxed and he caught her gaze in the reflection.

He didn't want her stressed out at the thought of facing her family. "Believe me. The most anyone will think is we had a quick make-out session. That's not so bad is it?"

She stroked her fingers over his arms that circled her waist. "No. That's not bad at all. *This* isn't bad. I'm just…"

"I know." He breathed in the scent of her hair. "That's why I couldn't touch you just now. I'll make it up to you later, Scarlett. Everything you want. All night long."

There was no hint of tension in the gorgeous smile she gave him. "You've already given me everything I want."

He had no idea what she meant, but it sounded good. "Ready to face the world?"

She took a deep breath and then nodded. "Yes."

He slowly released her and stepped back. *I want to take you home.* Right now. At least she no longer looked on the point of freaking out. He just had to suck it up for a few more hours.

No problem.

She turned around and faced him. "Let me have a look outside and see if anyone's nearby." Then she caught sight of the towels on the floor and hastily slung them into a laundry chute.

"I've got a better idea. You go out through the house, and I'll leave the way we came in. That way even if anyone's spying on us they won't get any incriminating photos."

She laughed and patted his chest, her hand lingering there for a moment. "Good thinking. If I didn't know better I'd think you'd done this kind of thing before."

He tugged her hand up and kissed the tips of her fingers. "Nope. This is all new for me, babe."

Her lips brushed his. "See you on the other side."

He waited until she closed the door behind her before stepping outside.

To find Edward Saunders glaring at him.

Chapter Nineteen

Jackson ignored the other man. The afternoon was too good to ruin by acknowledging the jerk's hostility. He strolled in the direction of the bar.

Saunders stepped into his path. "Having a good time, Grayson?"

It was hard to ignore someone when he shoved his ugly mug right into his face. Jackson stared him down for a few moments, easy enough to do, since he was a good four inches taller.

Finally, the other man dropped his gaze and Jackson waited for him to get out of his way. But Saunders didn't move.

What the hell was it with this guy? "You got a problem with me? Aside from the fact I'm holding up your precious redevelopment?"

Saunders gave a tight smile. "I'm not concerned with your paltry efforts to delay progress. But I do object to the way you're attempting to use Scarlett to further your cause. It won't work."

What the fuck? That was the second time in two days he'd been accused of using Scarlett for her connections. He forced a smile to his face, and took savage satisfaction at the way Saunders took a hasty step back. Clearly Jackson's smile conveyed how much he'd like to shove the weasel through the nearest window.

"You might use women for your own ends, Saunders. Doesn't mean all men do."

Saunders sent him a twisted smile from the safety of three feet away. "I've seen her name on the petition, Grayson. I keep my ear to the ground and I know she's sounding out her sources for you. Just how low can you sink?"

Scarlett had signed the petition? Why hadn't she told him? He'd not looked at it in weeks. And what the hell did Saunders mean by she was sounding out her sources?

Saunders might by lying through his teeth. But his gut reaction knew the other man was speaking the truth.

An odd constriction tightened his chest. It had never crossed his mind Scarlett would get involved. The possible loss of the dojo was his problem. He hadn't even asked her yet if she had any ideas for helping to get the word out on saving Heyward Street from demolition.

He refocused on the man in front of him. He'd love nothing better than to wipe that sneer off his face with a well-placed fist. But the days were long gone when he solved his arguments with violence.

"Here's the difference between us." He was impressed by the even tone of his voice. "I don't use women in that way. Whatever Scarlett does, she does because she wants to.

Is that clear?"

"Don't give me that crap. Scarlett's besotted with you. She'll do anything for her bit of rough from the wrong side of the tracks. But that novelty will wear off soon enough."

Who the fuck did this little shit think he was? Jackson had moved toward him before he even realized, and only the flash of triumph on the other man's face pulled him up short.

Saunders 1. Grayson 0.

He wouldn't let that happen again.

"You think?" He ground the words between his teeth.

"No I don't *think*. I know. Do you really imagine the Ashfords would allow something like you into their ranks? When it really counts, Scarlett isn't going to choose you above them. She's just having fun with you. Shame you seem to think it's something more."

Don't rise to the bait. Blood thundered against his temples, drowning out the distant sounds of the party. It was obvious Saunders was begging for a fight. And damn him, he was pressing all the hot buttons with his remarks. Because wasn't that exactly what Jackson was afraid of, deep inside?

That Scarlett was only with him for a bit of fun?

A month ago that was all he wanted. He would never have guessed so much could change in four short weeks.

He battled against the primitive urge to settle this score the way he would have ten years ago. What was it about Edward Saunders that made him want to undo all the years of training he'd undertaken?

"There you are, Jackson." Scarlett's voice broke into his thoughts and gave him the answer to his question. The acidic knot in his chest eased and he looked her way.

Her father was by her side.

"Dad, I never got the chance to formally introduce you before. This is Jackson Grayson. Jackson, this is my dad, Marshall Ashford."

What were they supposed to do, shake hands? Jackson very nearly just jerked his head in the older man's direction, but dismissed the idea instantly.

Everyone at this barbeque except for Scarlett thought he was an asshole. So he stuck out his arm, and after a barely perceptible pause, Marshall Ashford took his hand.

"Pleasure." Jackson's voice was neutral. Ashford's grasp verged on brutal.

"Likewise."

Jackson couldn't figure out Ashford. If it had been anyone other than Scarlett's father, he'd think the man was enjoying this encounter.

"You can let go of each other now." There was an edge to Scarlett's voice and since Ashford appeared to have no intention of releasing his hand first, Jackson decided to be the bigger man and concede.

But only because Ashford was Scarlett's father.

"Wonderful barbecue, Mr. Ashford," Saunders enthused. What a fucking ass-licker.

"Should be, considering how much it cost."

"Can't beat good quality." Saunders cast a pointed glance in Jackson's direction.

"Agreed," Ashford said and Saunders looked ready to kiss the older man's boots. Jackson recalled Scarlett once saying that her being with Edward would make her dad's day. How could Ashford want someone like Saunders for his daughter? It was disgusting, and not just because of the sex aspect.

"Mr. Ashford, there's something I've been waiting to run by you. It's to do with—"

"I'm not discussing business today." Ashford gave Saunders one of his cold smiles. Could he give any other kind?

"Of course not. Absolutely. Another time then."

Ashford turned to Scarlett. "Don't forget to introduce your friend to your uncle, honey. I know he'd like to meet him."

From her father's tone Jackson could just imagine how much the elder Ashford would like to meet him.

"Sure." Scarlett looked at Jackson and gave him a smile that stabbed straight through his chest. Was she really oblivious to what her father thought of him? *This isn't still all a game to her.* Not the way it had been on the night of her father's wedding.

Ashford strolled off. Saunders inched closer to Scarlett and Jackson stiffened. *Any closer, buddy…* He snapped the thought off before it could finish. Because there was only one way it could finish, and that was in him spilling Saunders' blood.

The thought was way too appealing for comfort.

"Haven't you met Crispin yet then, Jackson?" There was a false note of friendliness in Saunders' voice. He'd obviously changed tactics now Scarlett was on the scene.

"Oh, I didn't know you were on first name terms with my father's brother." Scarlett smiled, innocence dripping from every word, and Jackson coughed to mask his snort of laughter. She might be too nice to cause a scene in public, but this was the second time she'd put Saunders in his place.

Saunders grimaced through his teeth. It was obvious Scarlett's put down rankled, and Jackson took an instinctive step closer to her. Just because she was capable of standing up for herself didn't mean he had any intention of standing by and letting her. *If you even think about insulting her, it's me you'll be dealing with.*

"Jackson and I were having a chat before you arrived," Saunders said, obviously deciding to ignore Scarlett's last comment. Although why he'd want to tell her about their *chat* was beyond Jackson.

Scarlett shifted her weight from one foot to the other. She might look fine, but that little shuffle was a dead give-away. To him, at least. She wasn't comfortable talking to Saunders, but she wouldn't tell him where to get off. Would she kill him if he did it for her?

"Really?" Her voice was so polite it hurt his eardrums.

Saunders smiled, like a snake about to strike. "That must be some retainer you have him on."

The silence after that remark drummed through his head. And then both he and Scarlett spoke at the same time.

"Excuse me?'

"Watch your fucking mouth."

He saw the stricken look on her face before she managed to recover herself. Rage pumped through him at how easily Saunders had managed to hurt her. It didn't matter that what he said was a pile of shit. There was a grain of truth buried in there, and that was why he was so fucking mad.

"I'm sorry." Saunders made a great show of looking shocked. "Was it some kind of secret, Scarlett? As far as I'm aware, it's common knowledge that you hired Jackson for your father's wedding. And then, of course, for the ball."

Jackson watched the blood drain from Scarlett's cheeks. But she didn't tell Saunders to go fuck himself. Didn't tell him he had no idea what he was talking about. She looked completely mortified, and the primal need to protect her from this vindictive asshole surged through him and he stepped in front of her.

"You need to check your sources before you start throwing allegations like that around."

"My sources are solid." Saunders sounded infuriatingly calm. Unlike Jackson, who sounded damn near rabid. "You on the other hand, should start worrying about the integrity of your business dealings. Your judgment would be compromised if matters went to court."

Right now Jackson didn't care about the threats against *Graysons'*. Or the possibility of losing the dojo to Saunders' redevelopment plans. Only one thing thundered through his head. "You leave Scarlett out of this, you prick."

"So eloquent. Is that what Scarlett sees in you?"

"For God's sake, Edward." Scarlett's agonized whisper tore through Jackson as she came to stand by his side. "What are you *doing*?"

"Don't worry your pretty head about it, sweetheart." Saunders spared Scarlett a brief glance and his patronizing tone scraped Jackson's nerves like fingernails along a chalkboard. "The men are talking."

"*What*?" Scarlett sounded more flabbergasted than furious.

Blood pounded against Jackson's temples. No one spoke to Scarlett like that. No one.

"Why don't you go find your father? I'll be right along, sweetheart."

She was not Saunders' sweetheart.

"No, I'm not going anywhere."

"It's for your own good. Your father doesn't want you associating with these kinds of people." Saunders grabbed Scarlett's arm and pulled her toward him.

What the *hell* did he think he was doing?

"Let go of her." Jackson didn't recognize his voice. But he recognized the fury bubbling deep in his gut.

Saunders ignored him. "Come with me, Scarlett."

"Edward. You're *hurting* me."

You're hurting me. Jackson was flung back in time, to when he and his brothers had huddled together on the top stair of their old house. Down in the kitchen their drunk father used his fists on their mom, while she cried and pleaded with him to stop.

You're hurting me. He, Alex, and Cooper had stared at each other. They'd been too little to help. Too terrified to move. He hadn't been able to help his mom. Hadn't been able to defend Cooper.

He'd never had the chance to tell his father what he thought of him.

A red haze filled his vision. All he could see was Scarlett trying to free herself from Saunders's grip, and the way the other man ignored her.

He didn't have the words. He never had the fucking words. But even as the thought pounded through his mind, his fist connected with the other man's face. Saunders dropped like a stone to the ground, blood dripping from his nose.

Scarlett's horrified gasp slammed him back to the present. *What the hell had he done?* He unlocked his fist and flexed his fingers, and fought the suicidal urge to follow Saunders onto the ground and beat the fucking shit out of him.

From the corner of his eye he knew Scarlett's family was moving toward them, like vultures drawn to a recent kill. But he couldn't drag his gaze away from the man on the ground, or miss the hint of a triumphant smile that Saunders quickly hid.

"Blood will out." Saunders' voice was low, but the mocking tone was unmistakable. "Like father like son."

It was a punch to the gut. He looked at Scarlett and she was staring at him, pale and wide-eyed, as though she had never seen him before. Something ugly twisted through his heart. Condemning glares burned through him from everyone, but none of them mattered.

Nothing mattered, except for the way Scarlett stood there, frozen in shock, because she had finally seen him for who he really was.

There was nothing Jackson could say to her. All his years of trying to bury his past, of trying to prove to himself that he was better than his father, had been destroyed with one angry punch.

No words could undo his actions. He didn't have them in any case. *Eloquence.* That was something he'd never possessed.

All he possessed was the ability to settle a score with his fists.

A deathly silence had fallen. He had the insane vision of grabbing Scarlett's hand and ripping her away from her family, from this life, from everything she had ever known.

To be with him.

What a fucking joke.

He turned and walked away. No one tried to stop him.

No one said a word.

Not even Scarlett. Especially not Scarlett. And her silence cut through him more keenly than the knife that had once threatened his life.

Chapter Twenty

Scarlett watched Jackson turn and walk away from her. Without saying a word. But what could he say? That this was all her fault?

Guilt coiled through her. If she'd had the guts to tell Edward to back off weeks ago, this never would have happened.

She'd never forget the way Jackson had looked at her before he'd turned his back. There had been a strange blankness in his eyes, as though, finally, he'd seen her for what she really was.

A spineless coward. Too afraid to stand up for herself in case she upset her dad.

She let out a ragged breath and slowly turned back to Edward. He was laboriously getting to his feet, aided by a member of staff, and her entire family formed a giant semicircle around Edward and her, as though they were a shocking form of entertainment.

"I can't apologize enough." Edward dusted down his

pants and addressed himself to her dad and uncle. The two men stood shoulder to shoulder, as they always did when they confronted the outside world.

Resentment stirred deep in her gut. They would take Edward's side in this because Edward was related to Clarissa, and Clarissa was now an Ashford. And nobody fucked with the fucking Ashfords.

"What happened?" Her dad's voice was deceptively calm, but she knew him too well to be fooled for a second. He was mad as hell.

"I don't know." Edward spread his hands in an expressive gesture of perplexity. "I was simply saying how I didn't approve of the way he was using Scarlett for his own ends, and he attacked me without provocation."

Everyone looked at her. Her face burned. Did they all know she had bought Jackson's services for her father's wedding? Did they all think she'd been paying him to sleep with her for the last month?

For a second the prospect paralyzed her. All her life she'd kept to the shadows, happy to stay out of the limelight and the gossip pages. Obscurity had been her refuge after her mom had died, and all she'd wanted ever since was for her dad to truly notice her again.

He was noticing her now. His entire attention was focused on her, despite the way Edward kept babbling on about what a loose cannon Jackson Grayson was, and how *horribly worried* he'd been about Scarlett's wellbeing.

And then fury streaked through her, incinerating her shame. *So the hell what if she* had *hired Jackson to be her own personal sex slave?* It was nobody else's business.

"Shut up." She shot the words at Edward, and he shut up

mid sentence, a look of astonishment on his face.

Everyone stared at her. She couldn't have put herself more in the center of attention if she'd stripped naked and performed an erotic dance around the flagpole.

She didn't care. Let them stare. She'd had enough of taking everyone's crap.

"Scarlett, sweetheart." Edward's use of the endearment made her flesh crawl. "You must see what he's like now. A man without integrity. You'd never be safe with him."

A chill inched over her arms as Edward's meaning finally clicked into place. He wasn't acting this way simply because he felt slighted by her refusal to date him. It was all a ploy to try and get her father onside in his battle with Jackson over the redevelopment of Heyward Street.

She took a step toward him. "Jackson has more integrity than any other man I know."

For a moment Edward's mask slipped. He recovered instantly, and leaned in close. "Not by the time I've finished with him. I'll sue his ass off for this assault, Scarlett. He'll be lucky to keep a shirt on his back, never mind his precious slum."

Scarlett hadn't gotten involved in the family business by choice. But she'd lived on the sidelines her whole life. She knew how things worked. Knew who pulled the strings and which palms were regularly greased.

She never thought the day would come when she would be willing to use that information.

Guess what, asshole? That day has come. Maybe she was more like her father than she imagined.

She tilted her head and looked Edward straight in the eye. "You do that." There was a thread of steel in her voice, and it wasn't just Edward who stiffened in shock. From the corner of her eye she saw her dad tense. "And I'll ensure every official you've bribed so far is named and shamed. Don't believe I can't do it. It's a juicy story just begging to be spilled."

Silence thundered. It seemed her entire family held their collective breath, although surely it was impossible they had all heard her threat. Her chest tightened, suffocating her, and she abruptly turned away from the slack-jawed disbelief on Edward's face.

She doubted he would sue Jackson. Not now. But if he did, she would follow through. Even if it meant fighting her father in the process.

The Ashford media empire might be the biggest dog in town. But it wasn't the only one.

She kept her head up and spine straight as she stalked back to the house. *Thank you boarding school.* No one would guess that all she wanted to do was find a dark corner and hide.

Just like I always hide from everything. If she'd told Edward to fuck off, the way she'd wanted to earlier today, none of this would've happened. But it had. Jackson had left. And taken her heart with him.

Oh God. Her stomach churned and she blinked back the tears stinging her eyes. Why hadn't she ever told him how much he meant to her? She thought they had plenty of time to talk about *feelings.* But there was never enough time for things that really mattered. Now she might never get the chance.

As she reached the house, her father called her name.

I'm not talking to you.

She increased her pace. Nothing mattered but finding Jackson and trying to… Trying to what? Persuade him she was worth taking a second chance on? Would he even want to see her again, never mind speak to her?

He'd worked so hard to put the violence of his past behind him. She couldn't imagine how he must be feeling now.

I'm not responsible for Edward's behavior. Would Jackson see that once he'd had time to think about it?

"Scarlett." Her dad's voice was right behind her. Why couldn't he take a hint? She stopped by the open French doors, took a deep breath, and faced him.

"That was some performance." His voice was level and she couldn't see his eyes, hidden as they were behind designer shades.

Not that it mattered. His eyes would be as cold as the smiles he bestowed on her.

"That was no performance, Dad." For ten years she had agreed with every word he said to her. For the last eighteen months she'd tiptoed around him, in fear for his life. But she had been wrong. Her father wasn't a fragile flower clinging onto life by a slender thread. He had fully recovered his health and strength, and deep inside she'd always known it.

It had simply been another excuse to blind herself to the truth. To the fact that even in full health, he would rather keep her at arm's length.

He pulled off his shades. It had to be a trick of the light, because it seemed a gleam of warmth lurked in his eyes.

"You told me it wasn't serious between you and

Grayson."

"It wasn't. But now it is." Why had it taken something like this to make her see just how serious it was? *Suppose Jackson hates me now?*

"I warned you he could break your heart." Was that a thread of sympathy in his voice? Surely not.

She folded her arms, couldn't help herself, even though it told her father a whole lot more than any number of denials.

"He didn't break my heart." Not yet. But she had the despairing feeling that he might, and soon.

He didn't say anything for a few moments. And then he gave her an odd look. "You reminded me so much of your mother just now, the way you stood up to Saunders like that."

It was the last straw. She glared at him, and all the rejection and frustration she had buried over the last ten years bubbled to the surface.

"I'm not Mom, Dad. I never have been and I never will be. I can't help the way I look."

He frowned, but it wasn't one of his dismissive, I-don't-have-time-for-this-crap frowns. He seemed genuinely confused.

"I know you're not your mom, honey. But you looked just like she did, that day she stood up to her dad and told him I was the only man for her."

Scarlett knew all about that story. She wasn't interested in going over ancient history and had no idea why her dad thought now was a great time to reminisce.

"Would it help if I dyed my hair red?" She grabbed a handful of her hair and waved it at him. "Or what about a nose job? Then could you stand to look at me for more than five minutes without wishing I was *her*?"

A stricken look flashed over his face. It was gone in an instant but it was enough to drive a shaft of guilt deep into Scarlett's heart. She should apologize to him. But the words stuck in her throat.

Her dad wasn't the only one who still missed having her mom around.

"I've never wished you were her." There was a catch in her dad's voice that was so unlike him Scarlett bit her lip and dropped her gaze. "But after she died I just didn't know how to cope with you. You and your mom were always so close."

"You didn't have to pack me off to boarding school." The accusation was out before she could stop it. But why shouldn't she tell him how she felt about that? He had discarded her broken heart as though she was nothing but an inconvenience in his life.

"I'm sorry." His voice was low and shock ricocheted through her. Marshall Ashford never apologized. He might issue retractions or withdraw thinly veiled allegations, but he never apologized. "It was wrong of me to send you away, Scarlett. And when you came back you were so distant I thought I'd lost you forever."

She didn't know what to say. Never in a million years had she dreamed of having a conversation like this with her dad. And all because she had publicly defended the man she loved. Because of course she loved Jackson. *Guess I fell for him that very first night.*

"You didn't lose me." How ironic that after so many years of wanting her dad to open up to her, now that he was, all she could think about was leaving to find Jackson.

Her dad caught sight of her arm and his expression

hardened. She followed his gaze and saw bruises forming from where Edward had grabbed her.

"Don't worry about Saunders." There was a deadly note in her dad's voice now. "He's about to fall from a very great height."

"I'm not worried about him. But Clarissa might not like his fall from grace."

"I can handle Clarissa."

She guessed he could. *Why did I ever think Clarissa had the upper hand?*

"I presume you're off to find Grayson."

Her stomach pitched with nerves. She had to find him. But she wasn't exactly looking forward to the confrontation. *What if he never wants to see me again?*

"Yes. I don't think I'll be back for the fireworks." If Jackson forgave her, she'd never expect him to spend time with her family again. And if he rejected her, there was no way she could face anyone tonight.

"About this redevelopment. Let me know what I can do to help Grayson."

Scarlett stared at her dad in shock. Although his tone was casual, it wasn't an offer made lightly. It was an olive branch. A tacit acceptance of Jackson in her life.

For a moment she was tempted. The Ashford pockets were infinitely deeper than anything Edward Saunders could lay his hands on. With the empire on Jackson's side, he was guaranteed to win against the planned redevelopment.

But he wouldn't want that. And the truth was—neither did she.

"Thanks." She touched her dad's hand and he caught her fingers and held onto them. "But no thanks, Dad. Jackson doesn't need that kind of help. We'll do it our way."

We'll do it our way. The words spun around her mind in a never ending loop as she drove away from her dad's. She'd do it any way Jackson wanted, if only he gave her the chance to make things right with him.

But first she had to find him.

He wasn't at his house or the *Graysons'* office. At least, she couldn't see his car anywhere and there was no answer when she rang the entry bell. She sat back in her car and gripped the steering wheel.

She could call him. It was the obvious answer. But she had the feeling he wouldn't pick up. And although she could send him a text, that was taking the easy way out.

She was done with taking the easy way out. He could be anywhere. The chances of her finding him weren't great. There was only one other place she knew of where he might likely be. His dojo.

She took a deep breath, which did nothing to calm the nerves churning her stomach, and pulled out onto the road.

Chapter Twenty-One

In the gloom of his office at his dojo, Jackson popped the cap on the third and final bottle of beer that had been stashed in the trunk of his car. It wasn't nearly enough to give him a buzz, let alone dissolve the hard rock lodged in his chest, but there were no shops open locally to buy some more.

It was going to be a very long, shitty night.

Sprawled in his chair, one foot propped on an open desk drawer, he contemplated the framed certificates on the wall. He'd worked so damn hard to channel his anger and curb his instinct to use his fists. Passing each grade had given him a quiet sense of pride, and the conviction he was able to leave his past behind him.

To leave his father's shadow behind him.

But he couldn't. Because that darkness was inside him, and it had cost him the woman he wanted most in the world.

Someone knocked on the front door. He ignored it and took a long swallow of warm beer. The dojo was shut. Any fool could see that.

The fool knocked again, harder this time, and then followed it up by rapping on the front window with what sounded suspiciously like keys.

A dull sense of anger washed through him. All he wanted was to be left alone to wallow. Except he didn't have enough booze on hand to wallow in, which was a major pain in the ass. He scowled and pushed himself to his feet. Whoever was at the door had better be ready to run.

He unlocked the door. Cooper stood there, pulling his helmet off. "What the hell are you doing here?" He was in no mood for Cooper's brand of humor right now.

"Looking for you." Cooper pushed past him and Jackson gritted his teeth before he slammed the door shut. "I was on my way to the Ashford's but saw your car as I was passing."

"You were on your way *where*?" Jackson stared at his brother in disbelief.

"If you don't answer your cell, how the fuck else can I get hold of you?"

Far as he knew, Cooper had called him once today. He hadn't bothered replying to the subsequent text since he'd been late getting to Scarlett's.

"You'd never get through the gates." And neither would he anymore.

Cooper grinned. "Sure I would. My legendary charm works wonders."

It wasn't worth arguing that point. "Don't tell me Alex sent you." His older brother might still be pissed with him for not showing up to their gran's, but it wasn't like him to grind an ax when the moment had passed.

"Nah. I need a favor. I've had an emergency job come

up this week. Can you cover for me?"

"If I'm free."

"You are. I checked."

Jackson didn't feel that deserved any response, and took a long swallow of beer. Cooper didn't take the hint, and instead a frown crossed his face.

"What're you doing here anyway?"

"What's it look like?" He turned and made his way back to the office. Cooper once again didn't take the hint and followed him.

"Scarlett Ashford dump you?" Cooper leaned against the wall and grinned, as though he'd just cracked a joke.

Jackson's grip tightened around the bottle. "Don't go there." His voice was harsh. Scarlett had no need to dump him. His actions had done that without her needing to say anything.

Cooper's smirk faded. "What happened?"

"Don't start. Alex told me weeks ago what a fucking dick I am."

"Course you're a fucking dick. But I'm not Alex. And I've never heard you talk about a girl the way you did about Scarlett the other day."

Jackson stared at his brother. "I didn't say anything about her."

"You basically said you were seeing her. As in *seeing her*."

"Whatever. I'm not *seeing her* anymore."

"Family gave her the ultimatum, huh?"

Jackson slung his brother an irritated look. He'd always known the Ashfords didn't think he was good enough for Scarlett. But it was something else knowing his brother thought the same.

"They didn't have to. I lost my temper. Hit one of the bastards. I think it's safe to say that's the end of Scarlett and me."

"You hit her dad?" Cooper sounded torn between admiration and disbelief.

"Of course I didn't hit her dad. It was some dickwad who couldn't keep his hands to himself."

"And Scarlett dumped your ass for that?"

No she hadn't. He hadn't given her the chance.

"Are we done?" He waved his beer in the direction of the door. Cooper ignored him.

"You haven't been in a fight in over eight years. You have shit timing, bro."

"Thanks for pointing out the fucking obvious."

Cooper put his helmet on the desk. "When was the last time you got into a fight over a girl?"

He'd never been in a fight over a girl. If a girl wanted that kind of attention then she could move on to the next mug.

Jackson glared at his brother. "What's your point?"

"You really care about Scarlett Ashford."

"Give me a break." He growled the words as denial thundered through his brain. But what was the point. He did care about Scarlett. But if Cooper laughed, then God help him. "The jerk was hurting her."

The smug expression on his brother's face faded. "Okay. I get that."

There was a silence. Jackson stared at his beer, but it had lost its appeal. "I didn't want her to see that side of me, Coop."

"You had reason. Back then and now."

Jackson rocked the base of the beer bottle on his desk. "He's a mouthy bastard. If I had the words... but I don't. I never have. You talk a lot of shit but at least that keeps you out of trouble."

"Not always."

Jackson knew what Cooper was thinking about. "You were just a kid. Our dad was a prick." Jackson heaved a sigh. "We're so fucked up."

"Speak for yourself." Cooper offered him a half-grin. "There's no chance she'll take you back? When she's had time to cool off?"

Jackson focused on the toe of his boot. "She didn't dump me. I walked out of there. She didn't try and stop me." Of course she hadn't. Why would she? She'd probably been thanking God for her lucky escape.

"So you're not finished." It wasn't a question.

"Good as." Jackson pushed himself to his feet and prowled the length of the small office. "She won't take me back now."

"How do you know?"

Jackson rounded on his brother, ready to give him a right mouthful, but Cooper wasn't grinning. He was frowning. That was so unlike Cooper, who sailed through life, treating it as a joke.

"What we had wasn't serious. We both knew that." Yeah, he'd been damn sure to lay out the ground rules, hadn't he? And then he'd been the one who wanted to change them.

"If this wasn't serious, why've you spent the last five minutes banging on about it?"

Fuck that. "I haven't been banging on about anything."

"Seems to me," Cooper said, "you're in love with Scarlett Ashford."

Cooper's accusation hit him right in the gut. He gave a mocking laugh to cover his shock. "Don't be a dick. Of course I'm not in love." Shit, he might've fallen for Scarlett but that wasn't love.

"Yeah. Keep telling yourself that."

It wasn't love. The words sounded hollow.

What was love anyway? He had no idea. But the thought of not seeing Scarlett again made his chest ache.

It was more than just sex. Why bother to deny it. He might as well be honest with himself, now, when it was too late to matter, because he'd never get the chance to tell her.

Just like he'd never get the chance to tell her that, after so many years of beating himself up over what had happened to Cooper, he'd finally accepted that it wasn't his fault, because Scarlett had forced him to face the truth of that night.

He gripped the edge of his desk with both hands and hunched his shoulders. "Shit."

Cooper slapped his back. "What're you going to do about it?"

He couldn't go back to Marshall Ashford's mansion. No way would they let him back in. They'd probably call the cops on him, if they hadn't already. "I shouldn't have bailed."

He should've stayed and faced the shit storm, tried to make Scarlett understand that wasn't who he was anymore. Fuck, he'd even apologize to that piece of shit Saunders if it meant Scarlett would give him a second chance.

"Guess not." Cooper sounded too damn cheerful, and Jackson glared at him. "You need a ride?"

No way did he want a ride with Cooper. But if he copped

a DUI that would really go down well in his plans to try and win back Scarlett.

He followed Cooper outside. His heart slammed into his throat. Scarlett was walking toward him.

He stared at her, speechless. She looked so out of place in her designer dress and spiky heels. Not like the time he'd brought her to see his dojo when he'd deluded himself that she fitted into his life just fine.

She'd always been out of his league. He'd just never wanted to face it before.

"Jackson." She smiled at him, but it wasn't one of the smiles that lit up her face. She glanced at Cooper, who was doing a bad job of trying not to stare at her. "Is this a bad time?"

He cleared his throat. "No." It was all he could manage. What the hell was she doing here? To warn him he could expect a ball-breaking lawsuit to land in his mailbox? Right now that probability was the least of his worries.

"Great timing," Cooper said, finally dragging his gaze from Scarlett. "Catch you later, J." He sauntered toward his bike.

"I didn't mean to interrupt."

Jackson shrugged. "You didn't. That was just Cooper."

He watched Scarlett take a deep breath, as though she needed courage to face him. Disgust coiled through him that Scarlett, of all people, should be afraid of him.

"I know you probably don't want to see me right now."

Was she crazy? Why would she think that?

"But I'd like to try and sort things out with you."

He was the one who needed to sort things out. He thought he'd have time on the way to the Ashford mansion to dig up the words he needed, but life was never that easy.

But at least here he didn't have her entire family watching him grovel. "Sure." He pushed the door open and waved her in.

"I just wanted to say…" Her voice trailed away. He folded his arms and leaned back against the door. He was afraid if he didn't, he wouldn't be able to keep his hands to himself. And if Scarlett pushed him away in disgust, the look on her face would haunt him forever. "The thing is—"

"No." Shit, this was hard. He didn't even know what to say, let alone how to say it. "Listen to me. There's something I have to tell you."

"Please don't, Jackson. Let me say what I have to first."

Every muscle in his body tensed. Just because she hadn't burst through the door raging in fury didn't mean she wasn't mad as hell. Scarlett didn't rant or physically attack. But she'd cut Saunders down to size with a few well-chosen words, and he had the feeling she hadn't even been trying very hard.

He'd rather she tried to scratch out his eyes than tell him what she thought of him. At least scratches would heal in time.

"Fine." He shrugged to show he didn't give a damn about anything she might say. Inside he died a little more.

If this is love, it sucks.

"Okay." From the corner of his eye he saw her flex her fingers in a nervous gesture. Did she think he'd ever hurt her? He'd cut off his hand before he raised it against her.

If she's so afraid of me, why did she come here alone?

"I'm sorry."

Her words penetrated his throbbing head, and he stared at her. She was sorry? What was she talking about? She swallowed, and looked as though she was about to bolt from the room. But she didn't. She stood her ground and held his gaze.

After a few agonizing moments, it occurred to him she was waiting for him to reply. He didn't have a fucking clue what to say.

"What?" It was a croak and far from eloquent.

She licked her lips. "For putting you in that position. It was my fault. I'm sorry."

He had no idea what she was apologizing for. "What was your fault?"

"If I'd had the guts to tell Edward to back off weeks ago, none of that today would've happened."

That didn't make any sense at all. "I was the one who hit the bastard, Scarlett. I knew damn well he was punching all my buttons, trying to get me to lose my temper. But I still fell for it."

"If you hadn't hit him, I'm pretty sure I would have."

He gave a bitter laugh. "No, you wouldn't. You weren't dragged up in the gutter like I was."

Silence greeted his comment. Scarlett didn't move but she gave him a weird look, as though she'd never seen him before.

"Well," she said at last, just when the silence became unbearable. "Edward won't be pulling any more tricks like that in the future, that's for sure."

He didn't need to. Saunders had achieved his goal of getting Jackson out of Scarlett's life.

"Bet your dad's happy." He couldn't help the bitterness in his voice. It didn't make it any easier knowing this was all his own damn fault.

"Why would you say that?"

"He's always wanted you to get together with Saunders. You told me that yourself the night of the wedding."

"No I didn't." She sounded confused. "*Oh…*"

Before he could respond she reached out to lightly touch him, and he saw her arm. Bruises were forming where Saunders had grabbed hold of her earlier and a black rage twisted through him. *I hope I broke that bastard's nose.* He only wished he'd smashed a few of those thousand dollar teeth as well.

"I thought Dad wanted me to be with a man *like* Edward." She drew her hand back from his arm, as though she had just realized what she was doing. "I guess I was wrong about that."

"No, I don't think you were wrong about that." She didn't know about the visit Marshall Ashford had paid him. And she never would. "I can't even blame him for not wanting you to be with me. If I had a daughter I wouldn't want her to take up with someone like me either."

To his disbelief Scarlett smiled. "I wouldn't let that bother you. My mom's dad didn't want her to take up with my dad, and look how that turned out."

Why was she telling him that? What did that have to do with anything?

But she obviously expected some kind of answer. "Hardly the same." Jackson might no longer live in the gutter, but he was light years away from being a billionaire with a finger in every pie in town.

"Thirty-five years ago my dad and uncle were only just starting out. My grandfather, on the other hand, was a big deal in Hollywood. He might have been a terrible husband but he doted on my mom. He threatened to cut all ties with her if she disobeyed him." Scarlett frowned, as though something had just occurred to her. "She told him to go ahead, and walked out of his house with my dad."

Jackson couldn't see Scarlett ever doing that to her father. Not for him, anyway. But she was obviously trying to prove a point. Problem was, he had no idea what that point might be.

"That's got nothing to do what happened today."

"I know. I was just trying to show you that my dad wasn't always…" Scarlett hesitated and then took a deep breath. "I thought you blamed me for what happened with Edward. I wanted to apologize and ask you if—if we couldn't try and work it out between us. But now I'm just not sure what you think. Jackson, why did you leave like that?"

She wanted to work things out between them? After what he'd done in front of her father?

Relief rolled through him. He hadn't even needed to grovel for Scarlett to be willing to give him another chance.

"It was either that or wait until your father's heavies slung me off the property." That was one indignity he'd never be able to live down. But it wasn't the whole truth. He didn't want to tell her the rest. There wasn't any need because *she* had come to *him*, and she didn't think he was a no hope loser who couldn't keep his temper in check. But deep in his gut he knew he had to. "I didn't think you'd want me to hang around after you saw my true colors."

"I thought you left because you'd finally seen *my* true colors."

"Are you crazy?" All the things she'd said over the last few minutes finally made sense. "Nothing that happened today was your fault. It was between Saunders and me. I was on my way back to your dad's when you turned up."

"You were?"

"I needed to see you. I know I shouldn't have hit him." He glanced at her bruised arm, and the anger stirred again. "But you know what? If he ever hurt you again I'd do the same."

She took a step toward him. "So you didn't break up with me?"

He couldn't believe this conversation. He speared his fingers through her hair and forced her head back. Her lips parted and her palms flattened against his chest.

God, it felt good.

"Of course I didn't break up with you." He tried to focus, but it was hard when all he wanted to do was take her up against the door. "But where's this going, babe? What kind of future can we have?"

"Do you want a future with me?"

What kind of dumb question was that? Of course he wanted a future with her.

He wanted forever.

"Do you?" His voice was guarded. Just because Scarlett hadn't ditched him didn't mean she wanted them to get serious. Not the way he wanted them to.

Silence stretched between them. She wasn't going to answer him. And that gave him all the answer he needed.

And then she whispered one word. "Yes."

Chapter Twenty-Two

Jackson bent his head. Nothing else mattered but having Scarlett in his arms again. But before they even kissed, reality intruded.

"You might change your mind once the shit starts flying."

"I can handle shit." She gave a twisted smile. "You don't mean literally, I hope."

"Saunders won't take this lying down." He had a double ax to grind now. Not only had Jackson assaulted him, he had also lost the fight to win Scarlett.

"Ah." For some reason Scarlett looked guilty. "I'm pretty sure he won't be pressing charges against you."

Her earlier comment echoed through his mind. *Edward won't be pulling any more tricks like that in the future, that's for sure.* But why would Saunders back off when he had the perfect excuse to crush Jackson into the ground?

"Why's that?"

"I might have threatened to expose his unethical

business practices to the media."

She'd done *what*? "You threatened him?" He wasn't sure he could wrap his head around that.

"Yes. I know it was pretty low, but the thing is, if he wants to play dirty when it comes to you, then so will I."

For a moment he was speechless. Scarlett had threatened Saunders—for *him*?

He cleared his throat. "I don't want you getting involved in my battles." But that didn't stop the warm glow inside him.

"I know." She patted her fingers against his chest. "It wasn't just for your benefit. I did it for me as well. He had it coming."

He laughed. It was unexpected, and a shit load of tension drained from him. "I always knew you'd put him in his place one day. Wish I'd been there to see it."

Scarlett linked her hands behind his neck and pressed her body against his. It felt like forever since she'd been in his arms like this, instead of hours. With one hand anchored in her hair he slid his other arm around her waist and held her close.

"There's something else."

He inhaled her scent and rubbed his jaw across her silky hair. He didn't care what else there was. This was all he wanted. He grunted and swung her about so she was the one with her back to the door.

That should tell her all she needed to know.

"Jackson." She wound her fingers in his hair and tugged. "My dad offered to help in the fight against the redevelopment. He—"

Her dad. The crazy notion that he might find his forever with Scarlett splintered into a thousand jagged pieces. There was no forever, not for him, with Scarlett Ashford.

He pulled back and looked at her. Her hair was messy, her face flushed, her breath uneven. It would be too easy to kiss her senseless. Make her his and forget about the outside world.

But how long would that last? Only until they both collapsed on the floor, sweaty and sated. The real world was always going to be just outside the door. But it was more than that.

Her father loomed between them, a hostile shadow she would never see.

"I don't want your father's help." Once again he saw the sneer on Marshall Ashford's face as the other man had told him to name his price. What new game was Ashford playing now?

Whatever it was, it made Jackson sick to his stomach that Scarlett had gotten dragged into it.

He didn't know how Scarlett would take his refusal of her father's sham offer, but he hadn't expected her to look as though his answer thrilled her.

"I told him that."

He dragged his dark thoughts back to the present. "You told him what?"

"That we didn't want his help."

Jackson gave a hollow laugh. "Bet that went down well." And when Scarlett had time to think about it, she'd realize what she'd done.

He couldn't compete with her father. But even if he did, and won, how could he stand to know he was the cause of the rift between them?

Ashford might be a dick. But he was still Scarlett's father

and she loved him.

"He was fine about it." And then she frowned as though something had occurred to her. "It was weird. I almost got the impression he knew you wouldn't want his help. I mean, he didn't push it. And that's not like my dad, now I come to think about it."

That was because Ashford already knew he couldn't buy Jackson off. "He won't like it." He shoved his hands into his pockets but couldn't bring himself to step away from Scarlett. "He'll never accept the fact I won't toe the Ashford line for him. I don't kiss ass, babe. I kick it."

She gave a faint smile. "He'll never admit it, but he likes it when people stand up to him."

Not when his daughter was involved. "I don't think so."

Scarlett stopped smiling and pushed at his chest with both hands. "Are you going to let my dad come between us?"

That was rich. "He's already between us. He'll always be there, Scarlett. You know that."

She shoved at his chest again. "Of course he will. If you let him. Are you going to let him, Jackson?"

What the fuck? He grabbed her wrists and pinned her against the door, her arms stretched above her head. "We're not talking about me."

"Oh, I think we are."

Her taunt wasn't only unexpected. It was an unbelievable turn on. It took him a couple of seconds to realize she wasn't messing with him. She was actually pissed off.

"He'll never accept me in your life. You might think it's fun now but that'll wear off, believe me."

A blush spread over her cheeks. He knew she was angry but it didn't stop him wanting to silence her next words with his mouth. Hell, why was he even having this conversation with her? Why couldn't he just take this for whatever it was and enjoy it for however long it lasted?

Because I want more than that.

"So you think I'm here now because it's all a bit of fun to me? That this is all just a game?"

"Isn't it?" The challenge hung in the air between them, and hurt flashed through her eyes before she managed to hide it.

"This is between you and me. Don't drag my dad into it. He'd never get involved in this side of my life."

She really didn't know her dad at all. But as he stared at her, he saw disbelief and then comprehension dawn. Too late, he realized she had seen the skepticism in his eyes.

"He came to see you." It wasn't a question. It was an accusation.

"It doesn't matter."

"The hell it doesn't." Horror replaced the fury. Not that her fury had been directed at him. He knew that. "He tried to bribe you to keep away from me, didn't he?"

He released her wrists and pressed his palms against hers. Compared to his, her hands were so small. If anyone looked through the window and saw them, they'd be justified in thinking Scarlett was in danger. He loomed over her. He was inches from crushing her against the door. But Scarlett wasn't the one in danger here.

He linked his fingers through hers. "Didn't stop me coming to the barbeque, did it."

She opened her mouth and then shut it again. Finally she let out an infuriated splutter.

"He did it. He actually did it. I can't believe he had the

nerve."

"I told you. I'd probably do the same in his shoes." It sucked but it was true. He might not think much of Ashford but he could see his point on this.

Scarlett dug her fingernails into him. "Yes, I'm sure you would. Two of a kind, you and him."

What the…? She couldn't be serious. "We're nothing alike."

"After my granddad tried to pay him off to keep away from my mom, oh my God." Scarlett tried to tug herself free, and he tightened his grip on her. She glowered at him. "That was one of my dad's favorite stories when we were kids. He used to joke he'd do the same to any guy he thought might try and steal me away, to test his loyalty toward me, and my mom would tell him to stop being such an ass."

That definitely wasn't the reason why Ashford had come to see him. There was no way he wanted Jackson in Scarlett's life.

And yet…

That secret smirk Ashford had cast his way as he'd left had lingered in Jackson's mind.

Because it hadn't made any sense. Not then. And now?

"Son-of-a-fucking-bitch." Her father had been testing him. Seeing if he could be bought off. And Jackson hadn't seen it.

"And you both pretended you'd never met when I introduced you." Scarlett struggled to free herself again, and then she kicked him on the shin. "What was that all about, some stupid macho point scoring thing?"

To hell with it. Jackson crushed her against the door. "Your father is a conniving bastard." If they had any chance of a future together, she might as well know what he thought of her old man.

"Well, that makes two of you." Scarlett's frantic wriggles were shredding his thought processes and playing havoc with his self-control. "Let go of me. I can't move."

He released her hands long enough to hoist her over his shoulder. He heard her sharp intake of breath and could imagine the disbelief on her face. He grinned and marched back to his office.

"Put. Me. *Down*." Each word vibrated with outrage.

He kicked the door shut and only then slowly allowed her to slide down his body until her feet hit the floor. He let go of her, but she didn't reel backwards or slap his face. She appeared lost for words.

It was now or never. He either told her how he felt or risked losing her over a stupid argument.

He was no good at saying how he felt. He'd never done it before. Didn't want to start now. But Scarlett wasn't just mad with her dad anymore. She was furious with *him*.

"Do you want to know why I didn't tell you about his visit, Scarlett? Because I didn't want to give him any power in our relationship."

He took a deep breath. That hadn't been too hard.

"Oh. We have a relationship, do we?" There was an un-mistakable thread of sarcasm in her voice, but at least she no longer looked on the verge of scratching out his eyes.

All this talking was killing him. But at least he didn't have to bleed out his heart in front of her father.

"Yeah, we have a relationship. We belong together. You got a problem with that?"

"And you have no intention of kissing my dad's ass."

From nowhere he remembered something she'd said the

first night they'd slept together. About how she used to fight off fortune hunters.

He thought she'd been joking. But she hadn't. How many slimy jerks like Saunders had tried to worm their way into her life, simply because of her family connections?

"I don't need your dad's network." *Say it.* His tongue stuck to the roof of his mouth and he had the alarming notion that the room was closing in on him. He took a deep breath. They were just words. "I only need you."

Her hostility faded. For a terrible second he thought she was going to cry. Fuck, what had he said? He thought he'd just been romantic.

"You idiot." She poked him in the chest with one finger and then flattened her palm against his heart. "You already have me."

A great weight lifted from his chest.

He pulled her close and buried his face in her hair. This was where he needed to be. This was home.

Finally she stirred. "You don't ever need to see my dad again."

Now there was a tempting thought. Except he'd never backed away from a confrontation before and he'd be damned if he started now. "Nah. I have no intention of letting you go to all the Ashford bashes without me by your side. So get used to it."

"At least Edward won't be going to any of them, if my dad has anything to do with it."

"Huh. Finally your dad and me agree on something."

She smiled and then walked her fingers up his chest. "So does this mean I'm your official girlfriend?"

His girlfriend. He'd never had a proper girlfriend before.

It sounded… weird. "I guess."

"Don't sound too excited. I might start getting ideas."

"You're my girlfriend." It still didn't sound right. Maybe he just had to get used to saying it.

There was something else he needed to say to her. It wouldn't kill him. But they were still the hardest words he'd ever said in his life. "I love you, Scarlett."

She sighed and wound her arms around his neck. "I love you too, Jackson."

Epilogue

Finally, they were having a proper date. Jackson glanced at the view of the lake outside the window. He'd booked them into a top hotel for the night, but instead of getting room service they were eating in the dining room.

So he could show off his girlfriend.

But the word still didn't feel right. And now he knew why. It was because he wanted Scarlett to be so much more than that.

He wanted Scarlett to be his wife. The thought terrified him, but not half as much as the thought of living without her.

"I'm really looking forward to meeting your gran on Sunday."

"You know she's going to grill you about your intentions toward me."

Scarlett laughed. "She can't be worse than my dad. Can she?"

"I think we should get my gran and your dad together in the same room."

"They'd probably kill each other."

She thought he was joking. He resisted the urge to tug at his collar. He had an ulterior motive for this date tonight, but despite the plan he'd been working on for the last couple of days, fucked if he knew where to start.

"I want to talk about planning an event." He let out a relieved breath. Now that he'd started, it shouldn't be too hard to keep going. But before he could get his shit together, Scarlett leaned across the table. She looked thrilled.

But he hadn't told her what he wanted yet.

"I'd love to help, Jackson. Any way I can. As you know, I have plenty of contacts that I don't mind ruthlessly using for my own ends."

He stared at her. "Right."

"I've never personally done anything like this before, but I know my friend Harley would love to be involved. If that's okay with you?"

He cleared his throat. "Like a rally or something to save Heyward Street, you mean?"

"Yes. Well, maybe not a rally…"

"Okay, good." It was great she was so keen to help. But he didn't want to talk about his dojo or Heyward Street tonight. He rushed on before she could jump the gun again. "I wanted to get your opinion on hiring somewhere for an upmarket party."

She nodded. "Okay. What do you have in mind?"

"Something classy. But down to earth."

"Sure." She didn't look at all fazed. "What else?"

He should just ask her straight out. Cut through all this

bullshit. He grabbed his glass and downed the wine, but it didn't help him find the words.

"Something romantic." He broke into a sweat and filled his glass up again. Scarlett looked as though she didn't understand the meaning of the word.

"Romantic? You're not talking about an event to help save your dojo, are you?"

"No." *I'm talking about you.* "It's something I know my gran would love."

"Oh." Scarlett flashed him a smile but it looked a bit off. "Well, sure. I can do romantic and classy and down to earth. No problem."

Jackson tried to remember the next stage of his plan, but couldn't. Things had gone much better inside his head. By now Scarlett had guessed what he was trying to do and had saved him the headache of having to spell it out in actual words.

"By Thanksgiving."

"Absolutely. Is it a special birthday for your gran?"

It took him a couple of seconds to figure out why she'd brought his gran into the conversation. "No. It's just something I know she'd love."

To see one of her grandsons get hitched. Fuck, he'd never thought he'd be in this position. But then, he'd never thought he'd fall in love. Suppose Scarlett didn't want him?

She might love him. She might be fine about them dating and showing the world they were together. But that didn't mean she wanted to go all the way and marry him.

"If it's a special Thanksgiving event, we'll have to move fast. Is this a surprise for her, or can I talk to her about it on Sunday?"

He should never have mentioned his gran. He eyed the wine. Another bottle probably wouldn't help him out of this mess.

He took a deep breath. This was more nerve racking than his first street fight.

"This is about us, Scarlett. To celebrate our wedding. If you'll have me."

She stared at him as if he'd just grown another head. Fuck. This wasn't good.

"Did you just propose to me?"

He swallowed. Why had he thought this was a good idea? Walking barefoot across red-hot coals seemed preferable. "Yeah."

This wasn't the reaction he'd expected.

"Well… sure." She gave a weird smile, as though she wasn't sure whether he was serious or not.

Why hadn't he gotten her a ring? He'd spent hours trying to find the perfect one for her. He'd known exactly what he wanted—a pink diamond because it all tied in with her ball and the charity she loved so much. He'd never even heard of pink diamonds before that night.

But there was no way around it. If he wanted to get her a pink diamond engagement ring he'd need to take out a second mortgage.

But a ring would've shown her he meant it. That he wasn't fucking about. This night was going to hell. He should've asked Cooper to write him a speech or something.

With a sinking feeling in the pit of his stomach, he pulled the small jewelry box from his pocket. Scarlett gave a silent gasp when she caught sight of it. Maybe she recognized the jewelers it came from. He half wished he'd left it in his pocket. It wasn't what she so obviously imagined.

He pushed it across the table. "It's not a ring." It was only fair to warn her. But more than that, he knew he'd hate to see the disappointment on her face when she opened it.

Slowly she opened the box. Her smile froze when she saw what was inside. And then her smile disappeared altogether and she looked as though she was about to cry.

He sat there like a fucking idiot. If he dragged her into his arms and held her tight she wouldn't thank him for drawing the entire restaurant's attention. He took another gulp of wine and tried to think of something deep and meaningful to say.

"It's a rosebud." He sounded crazy and desperate. "It's not a pink diamond. It's only crystal. But I thought—"

Scarlett flapped a hand at him and finally dragged her gaze from the crystal rosebud, which had reminded him of her when he'd seen it in a glass display case. There were tears in her eyes and her bottom lip wobbled.

He should really have gotten her a ring.

"I know what it is." Her voice was all choked up. "I know what it represents. I'm just… this is the best present anyone's ever given me."

He wasn't sure she meant it. Her reaction was freaking him out. "I can take it back. We can get a ring instead. It's just I can't—"

The words lodged in his throat as Scarlett stood up, came round the table, and cradled his face between her hands.

"Don't you dare take it back." Her whisper was soft and husky. "I don't need a ring, Jackson. Not when I have you. Only you would've thought to get me something so perfect. I love it. And I love you."

The knot in his chest eased. "So that's a yes, then? You're definitely going to marry me?"

"Yes, I am. There's no way you're getting out of that now. You just hired me to organize our wedding, didn't you?"

"Guess I did. Can I afford your rates?"

"I'm not sure. I might have to charge hazard pay."

He laughed before he could stop himself. Scarlett didn't seem to care that half the diners turned their way. "I knew you were trouble the second you walked into my office."

"That's right." She moved in close and kissed him. It was hard not to pull her onto his lap. "There's no escape for you now."

"I don't want to escape." He knew what he wanted. And she was in his arms. "I want forever."

THE END

Acknowledgments

As always a big thank you to my wonderful family for putting up with my distracted mind and all the late nights I spend in my own worlds. Thanks also to my awesome editor Candy Havens and everyone at Entangled Publishing who work so hard behind the scenes. And finally for my good friends Amanda Ashby and Sara Hantz - this journey wouldn't be half as much fun without you both!

About the Author

Christina Phillips is an ex-pat Brit who now lives in sunny Western Australia with her high school sweetheart and their family. She enjoys writing paranormal, historical and contemporary romance but whether the hero is a fallen angel, tough warrior or sexy mortal, the romance will be sizzling and the heroine will bring her hero to his knees. She loves hearing from her readers!

Christina is addicted to good coffee, expensive chocolate and bad boy heroes. She is also owned by three gorgeous cats who are convinced the universe revolves around their needs. They are not wrong.

www.christinaphillips.com